STOCKTON-ON-TEES BOROUGH LIBRARIES

BILLINGHAM LIBRARY
KINGSWAY
BILLINGHAM
TS23 2LN
01642 528084

A fine will be charged if this book is returned after the due date. Please return/renew this item by the last date shown. Books may also be renewed by phone or internet. Replacement charges are made for lost or damaged items.
www.stockton.gov.uk/libraries

Wild Thing

His leg was broken and his provisions were all on his horse. There was no way he could catch the horse on a broken leg. He was miles from any help, high up in an isolated mountain valley.

The only human being within miles was some wild girl he was seeking but she was suspected of two murders. Indeed, she had already tried to kill him twice.

With winter coming on, Deputy United States Marshal Carver Dilling weighed his chances. Perhaps the vicious Indian who also sought the girl would find him first. Not a pleasant prospect, but about the best he could expect.

At least he'd die fighting.

Wild Thing

BILLY HALL

A Black Horse Western

ROBERT HALE · LONDON

ISBN 0 7090 7667 3

Robert Hale Limited
Clerkenwell House
Clerkenwell Green
London EC1R 0HT

Typeset by
Derek Doyle & Associates, Shaw Heath.
Printed and bound in Great Britain by
Antony Rowe Limited, Wiltshire

CHAPTER 1

A whisper from another world, perhaps. A sense of some portent beyond his senses. Maybe a premonition. Possibly the stirring of some primeval inclination that his life was about to change.

Whatever it was crawled up the spine of Carver Dilling. He looked up from his battered desk. The Wyoming sun burned the street until even the dust felt hot. At this altitude it should be cool, even late in July. It wasn't. It was just plain hot. But it was more than unusually hot weather that pulled his lips into a thin line.

The feeling was familiar. Twice before its cold breath had stirred the fear he seldom felt. Twice before he had nearly lost his life. Only the extra vigilance the odd premonition spawned had made the difference between life and death.

This time it was stronger. It raised the hair on the back of his neck. It twisted his gut into a knot. His breath became suddenly ragged and thin, as if from too much exertion on some tall peak of the mountains.

He took a deep breath and let it out slowly. He moved from behind the desk on catlike feet, even in the thick leather, high-heeled boots of a working cowboy. He slipped his Colt .45 from its holster and checked its loads. He spun the cylinder. He checked the action of hammer and trigger. He slid it into its holster.

The feeling passed. The hard knot in his gut stayed. His fingers ran through the thick, black curls of his hair. For just a moment he longed for the simple work of a cowboy that he had known most of his life. That was before he pinned on this badge. Deputy United States Marshal. It used to sound romantic, important. Then he found that most of his job was routing paperwork, serving papers, filling out papers, storing papers, reading papers. The occasional bursts of excitement became welcome respites from the eternal paperwork.

Sometimes, though, life-threatening crises erupted in the middle of the boredom and tedium. It caught him napping the first time, and he almost died before he could change gears and react. He vowed never to do that again.

Except for the premonitions, he would have, though. It seemed impossible to stay alert all the time when his days were filled with boring, routine details.

This time he was ready. Well, he thought he was ready. Who could be ready for something with as many strange twists and turns as his life was about to take?

The office door burst open suddenly. Carver's hand streaked to his gun. With blinding speed, the .45 lifted and leveled. The hammer was on full cock, as if by itself. His finger poised on the trigger.

The young cowboy stopped so quickly he nearly fell. His eyes widened.

'Hold on, Marshal! I ain't. . . I mean, I didn't mean. . . My lord, Marshal, don't shoot me!'

Carver lowered the hammer and slid the .45 into his holster. His slow, soft voice contrasted starkly with the incredible speed of his draw.

'Sorry, Spud,' he apologized. 'You startled me a mite, poppin' in the door thetaway.'

'Yeah, I sorta noticed that,' Spud accused. 'You edgy or somethin'?'

'Well, I guess maybe a little. What can I do for you?'

'Will's dead.'

Carver frowned. 'Will who?'

'Will Tanning.'

'The homesteader up on East Fork?'

Spud nodded. 'That's him.'

'Accident, er somebody kill 'im?'

'Oh, it warn't no accident. His throat's slit from ear to ear. Blood all over. I ain't never seen that much blood in my whole life. Flies is blowin' it a'ready.'

'Who killed him?'

Spud looked at the marshal as if he didn't believe the question.

'Whatd'ya mean, "Who killed 'im?" '

'I mean, do ya know who killed him?'

'Well, I s'pose.'

Carver's voice betrayed impatience. 'So who do ya s'pose killed him?'

'Well, I s'pose it was that wild thing.'

'What wild thing?'

'You ain't heard?'

'I got no idee what yer talkin' about.'

'I s'posed 'most everyone in the country'd heard about it by now.'

'Heard about what?'

'The wild thing.'

'Well, I ain't. So how about ya tell me 'bout it, then we'll ride out there an' look the situation over. Did ya mess with anythin'?'

'I didn't touch nothin'. I wasn't about to wade through that blood, if I didn't have to. Besides, with that much blood all over, an' his head hangin' back over the back of the chair that way, I could see his head was cut 'most off. There sure wasn't nothin' I could do for him.'

'So what's this wild thing?'

Spud wiped his hand across his mouth. 'Well, better part of a month ago, Will, he went an' run on to a wild girl.'

'A wild girl?'

'Yeah. I'm pertneart sure that's what she is. She's sure 'nuff human, anyway.'

'Where'd he find her?'

'Well, he said someone slipped in one night an' stole some food out of his spring box. So he laid for whoever it was for the next several nights. Four or five nights later, she come in again. He caught her red-handed.'

'Stealing food.'

'Uh huh.'

'So what'd he do?'

'Well, he started talkin' to her, real quiet an' soothin' like. Sorta like he did to a raw bronc, you know. He had a way with horses, that man did. He could plumb talk a wild bronc into lettin' him crawl up in the middle of 'im, an' not hardly blow up atall on 'im. Real soothin' voice. Anyway, he said she run off a ways, but when he didn't chase her, she stopped an' listened. He talked her into sorta trustin' him.'

'She stayed with him?'

'Well, she never really stayed atall, I guess. He told 'er to take what food she needed. She didn't need to steal it. So she started comin' in durin' daylight even. Then he started tryin' to make friends with her.'

'Did he talk with her?'

Spud shook his head. 'Naw. He tol' me she never said a word. He wasn't sure she knew how to talk, or couldn't, maybe. She seemed to understand, though. Anyway, he got it in his head that he was gonna tame 'er. Make a civilized sort out of her. Said he thought he was gettin' the job done. Last time I talked to 'im, he said she'd even tried to warsh up some. He said she'd eaten at his table a time or two. Knowed how to use a knife an' fork, an' everythin'.'

'And you think that's who killed him?'

' 'Course it is! Who else would it be? I tried to warn 'im. I told 'im she was likely some Injun kid what got dumped an' growed up wild. When a human bein' goes wild, they're wild for good. Worse'n an animal. I told 'im, 'bout the first time he tried to touch her, she'd kill 'im. Just like a wild animal. Like tryin' to make a pet outa a cougar er somethin'. You think you've got 'im all tamed an' everythin', then he up an' eats one o' the kids.'

'She's Indian?'

Spud shrugged his shoulders. 'Will, he didn't think so. Said her hair was coal-black, though.'

'So's mine, but I ain't no Indian.'

Spud shrugged again. 'Yeah, well, I dunno. Anyhow, Will's plumb dead, an' she ain't nowhere around, o' course. Two an' two says she likely done it. Serves 'im right, I s'pose, fer tryin' to tame somethin' what ain't meant to be tamed. Still an' all, I'm gonna miss 'im. He was my best friend in the world, Will was.'

'He used to work for the U–Cross, didn't he?'

'Yup. Till he filed on that homestead. Still did work for Walt durin' roundup an' brandin'. Needed the extra money. Hard to start out from scratch, with just what he could save up from punchin' cows. He done good, though. Didn't never blow his money on booze an' whores like most of us. Saved it all, an' put it into that place. If he'da spent more of it on booze an' whores, maybe he wouldn'ta been so hard up he tried to tame that wild thing.'

'Maybe he just thought she needed help,' Carver countered. 'Humans aren't made to live wild like animals.'

'That's what Will thought, too. That's what got 'im killed.'

'Maybe,' Carver conceded. Mentally he was a long way from ready to make that assumption. 'Let's ride out an' take a look,' he said.

'You take a look,' Spud corrected. 'I already seen it once. Once is enough.'

Carver continued as if he hadn't heard. 'We'll take a buckboard, so I can haul his body back to town.'

Spud pondered a moment, then nodded. 'He deserves that at least. He deserves a Christian burial. But I can tell you for sure, that wild thing's gonna be shot on sight, like any rabid coyote.'

'If she's human, thet'd be murder,' Carver warned.

The chill that ran up his spine made him wonder suddenly what she really was. Human? Animal? Half and half? Some haunt, maybe? Who could know? Yet.

CHAPTER 2

'Don't be in there after dark!'

The words were as clear in Carver's mind as if they were audible. He shook his head, willing his childhood fear of ghosts and demons out of his mind.

'You say somethin', Marshal?'

Carver shook his head again. 'Nope.'

'I'll wait with the horses. They can smell the blood. Makes 'em nervous.'

'I'll be needin' ya to help me load 'im.'

'Yeah. I know. I ain't goin' in there till I gotta, though.'

Carver climbed down from the buckboard and looked around the yard. The house was small, but solidly built. Logs had been chosen carefully and trimmed to fit. Will must have been a good hand with an adze. He wasn't sure the logs even needed to be chinked. Two windows boasted real glass. The door swung easily on iron hinges.

Corral and shed were equally well built. The shed that sheltered his horses had room enough so that he could have had a milk cow too, if he managed to have a family some day.

In spite of the glass windows, the interior was dim. Carver waited to let his eyes accustom. Buzzing of countless flies filled his ears. As his eyes adjusted, it seemed as if the floor and table were alive. A solid mass of flies covered copious amounts of blood, dried black on top.

In the center of the pool of blood, Will Tanning still sat in the chair at his table. His head was tipped back. Way back. Back further than his neck would have permitted, normally. The front half of his neck simply wasn't there.

Carver stepped carefully around the pool of blood on the floor. He lit the lamp that still sat on the table. He replaced the chimney on it, then lifted it so he could see the dead man clearly.

Will's eyes were wide open, staring at the ceiling he couldn't see. His hands gripped the edges of the chair, beside his legs. His mouth gaped open. His throat was slit from side to side. Black, crusted blood was all that sealed it from being open all the way down.

'Sharp knife,' Carver muttered. 'One slice. Caught him by surprise. Just grabbed his chair to keep from falling over. Died afore he could figger out what happened, looks like. Sure sprayed blood all over afore he did, though.'

Carver looked around the room. Clothes were hung neatly on wooden pegs driven into the walls. A bed along one wall was neatly spread over with the blankets. A standing cupboard beside the stove held dishes, neatly stacked and clean. Curtains even graced the sides of the windows, without covering any part of the glass.

Will's pistol was still in its holster. His spurs were still on his boots. Twin furrows in the floor showed where his feet had shot forward, digging the spurs into the wood. They remained at the foremost end of the gouge.

'Come in fer somethin',' Carver muttered. 'Figgered on headin' back out. Otherwise he' da took his spurs off an' hung 'em up, neat as 'e was 'bout everythin' else.'

He pulled the large knife from its sheath on his belt. He squatted beside the deepest glob of blood on the floor. He carefully poked the knife into it, and lifted the crusted top.

'Dried half an inch down,' he muttered. 'Half a day. No more'n that, in this heat. Musta got killed less'n an hour afore Spud got here.'

He frowned, staring out the open door. He stood and walked outside. He took in several breaths of fresh air. He stepped back in and wiped the blood from his knife-blade on the dead man's trousers. He went back outside, sliding it into its sheath as he walked.

'Just like I told you,' Spud said.

Carver nodded. 'Ya got a knife, Spud?'

'What?'

'You got a knife? Ya carry a knife, don't ya?'

'Sure. Doesn't everybody?'

'Just about,' Carver agreed. 'Mind lettin' me see it?'

'You wanta see my knife?'

'Uh huh.'

'What for?'

'Just wanta look at it.'

Frowning, Spud slid the knife from his belt. He turned it over, holding the blade, offering it to the marshal handle first. Carver took it, looked at it closely, first on one side, then the other.

'What'cha lookin' for?'

Carver ignored the question. He held out his left arm. He positioned Spud's knife on his arm and drew it carefully toward himself, as if shaving his arm. The hairs on his arm remained intact.

'Ya don't keep it too sharp, do ya?' he remonstrated.

Spud shrugged. 'Aw, sharp enough to get me by. I ain't never been no hand at sharpenin' a knife. Some fellas, they sit around every evenin' stroppin' their knife on their boot-top. Or spittin' on a whetstone, if theirs are like mine, an' need more sharpenin' than a boot top'll give 'em. Me, I just never could make myself take that much time. I just work harder, when I gotta cut somethin'. It'll dress out a deer, though.'

Carver nodded, handing it back.

'I guess ya can help me haul Will out here. We'll drag him out of the blood, then wrap him in one of his blankets. Then we can throw him in the buckboard.'

'So what did you wanta see my knife for?'

Carver studied the cowboy closely for a long moment. His voice was still slow and steady as he said:

'Just wanted to be sure ya wasn't the one what killed him.'

Spud stared at the lawman with his mouth agape for several heartbeats.

'What? Me? Why would I kill Will? He was my best friend!'

Carver nodded. 'Sometimes friends argue,' he said.

Spud shook his head. 'Not me'n Will. We ain't never had words over nothin'. Well, 'cept that wild thing. He got kinda sore when I kept tellin' 'im to forget about tryin' to tame her. Other'n that, we never had a cross word.'

'Did ya ever see her?'

Spud shook his head. Then he said: 'Well, yeah. Sorta. Once. She's got ears like a deer. She was always long gone afore I even rode into the yard. Will always knowed when I was comin' if she was here, 'cause she'd light out like a streak. One time I sorta seen a movement in the brush behind the house when I rode in. Just a little glimpse. Like a blur, maybe. I figgered it was her, lightin' out. That's the closest I ever come to seein' her.'

'You know anyone that's seen her?'

'Couple o' the boys has. From a distance. Wilder'n a catamount, though. They didn't see much more'n enough to tell it was human.'

Carver nodded. 'Let's get it done.'

Spud still hesitated. 'So how'd you decide it wasn't

me that killed Will?'

Carver answered as he was walking back to the cabin.

'Your knife's too dull. Will's is still in its sheath. Whoever did it had a real sharp knife. Real sharp. Pertneart cut his head off with one swipe. If he'da hit between the vertebrae on his neck, instead o' hittin' bone, it likely woulda cut it clean off. Sharp knife.'

Spud swallowed hard. By the time he got to the door, Carver was backing out, dragging the dead man, chair and all. When he bounced the chair out the front door, he lowered it to the ground. Will's body remained rigidly as it had been. Carver could not let the chair clear on to the ground, because the weight would then rest directly on the top of Will's tilted-back head. He turned the chair over on to its side. The body toppled off it, but remained in the same position.

He walked back into the cabin and jerked a blanket off the bed. He spread it on the ground.

'Here, let's roll him over on to it.'

His face ashen, Spud grasped his friend's feet.

'You get his head,' he gritted.

Carver gripped the dead man by the shoulders, while Spud grasped the feet. Together they turned him over on to his back, then on to the other side. Carver wrapped the blanket around him as best he could.

'OK. Let's get him loaded.'

Gripping the blanket to avoid contact with the dead man as much as possible, they hoisted it and carried it to the buckboard. They heaved the macabre burden on to the bed of the conveyance. Carver shoved it forward far enough to be confident it wouldn't bounce out *en route* to town, then climbed back into the seat.

'Oughta shut the door,' Spud offered.

Carver shook his head. 'I'd leave it open. Animals will clean out the blood real well, if ya leave it open. Somebody might wanta live there, some day. Ya kin come by and shut it in a couple er three days, if'n it'll make ya feel better.'

Spud hesitated, then nodded. He climbed up beside Carver. Neither spoke for a long while. They were back to the main road by the time darkness settled. He let the horses move along at their own pace, knowing they could see better than he could.

They were back to Dubois when Carver said: 'Will have any family?'

'Not close,' Spud replied. 'Cousins, back in Indiana or somewhere. Why?'

'Oughta let somebody know.'

'Wouldn't know how.'

'Wonder who thet is?'

Spud squinted into the darkness. Somebody had lit the lamp in his office. In the glow that shone from the open door, he could make out the figure of somebody sitting in a chair on the sidewalk, just beside the door. 'Waitin' for you, looks like,' he offered.

'Looks like,' Carver agreed.

He pulled the team to a halt in front of the office.

'Howdy, Marshal,' the man called.

'Evenin',' Carver responded. 'You waitin' for me?'

'Yeah. Got to town a couple hours ago. They told me you'd gone out to Tanning's place, and would be back directly. Thought I'd wait. Will OK?'

Carver let the silence hang for a long moment before he responded. Then he said:

'Naw, cain't say he is. Somebody killed 'im.'

'Naw! You don't say! Will Tanning? How come?'

'Don't know.'

'Who?'

'Don't know thet either. What can I do fer ya?'

It took a long moment for the man to get his mind back on his business, and off his shock at the death of Tanning. When he did, he said:

'I, uh, had a horse stole.'

'Who are ya?'

'Oh. Sorry. Didn't think about it bein' too dark for you to see me. I'm Grant Tucker.'

Carver nodded in the darkness. 'You got a homestead on East Fork Crick.'

'Yeah. 'Bout five miles or so from Will. He's one o' my neighbors. Killed, you say!'

'When?'

'When was he killed?'

'No. When was yer horse stolen?'

'Oh. Yeah. Sure. My horse. Today. Heard 'im take off. Whoever stole 'im, took a bridle, but no saddle. Had 'im in the corral, right there by the house. Didn't hear nothin' till I heard Fred runnin' like everything.'

'Fred?'

'My horse. Name's Fred. Buckskin gelding. Five years old. Fine horse. Runnin' fool.'

'Ya chase 'im?'

'Naw. Only other horse I had in was Biscuit. She was in the shed. She couldn't catch Fred if Fred had one foot tied up. She's a good horse, but Fred . . . well, she ain't no match for him. Wasn't no sense gallopin' off after him on her.'

'So ya jist rode inta town.'

'Well, not straight away, no. Had some chores an' things to do. Come on in when I got done. Don't s'pose there's anything you can do about it, but I thought I'd tell you, just on the off-chance you'd run across him.'

'Branded?'

'Oh, yeah. Twenty-seven.'

'I remember seein' the brand. Left hip.'

'Yup.'

'The wild thing,' Spud said.

'What's the wild thing?' Grant asked.

'Stole your horse. Sure's anything. Killed Will, then stole your horse to get away.'

'That wild girl killed Will?'

'Nobody knows thet,' Carver insisted. 'All we know is somebody did. Spud says he was tryin' to tame some wild human animal what's been runnin' around the hills. He figures that's who killed Will. No evidence to support it, though.'

'How much evidence do you need?' Spud demanded. 'She slit his throat, run to Tucker's, stole a horse, an' lit out to the high mountains. It sure don't take a genius to figure that out.'

'Don't take a genius to be wrong, neither,' Carver countered. 'Why don't ya haul Will's body on up to the undertaker. Then ya kin take the buckboard back to the livery barn.'

'You gonna go lookin' for 'er?'

'I 'spect I'll try my hand at trackin' thet horse anyway,' Carver conceded. A voice in some hidden corner of his mind whispered, *Herrrr.* He shuddered in the dark as the cold fingers of that chill crept up his spine again.

CHAPTER 3

Dawn came two hours before the sun appeared. It was always that way, here in the mountains. The sky would lighten and the world would come alive. Then the night's chill would seem to deepen, instead of lifting. It would grow slowly lighter, with no abrupt changes. Then the sun would lift above the mountain range to the east, and light and life would seem to explode on every side. Trout came alive in the streams, and began to feed. The sun's hot rays drove away the chill of the night, making it feel even warmer than it was. Deer and elk sought sheltered copses of shade in which to bed down for the day. Men on the run began to look for places to hide until darkness wrapped its blanket of safety around them again.

Those first direct rays of sun found Carver Dilling already studying the tracks of a fleeing horse. The harshness of the light made tiny shadows at the edges of the hoof-prints, making the trail as plain as if drawn on paper. 'Good rider,' he mused. 'No saddle,

Grant said. Ridin' bareback, an' that horse was diggin' hard. Less of a rider would've been left sittin' on air, wonderin' where the horse went.'

He scowled at the trail as it led away into the distance. He looked around at the mountains that walled both sides of the narrow valley. East Fork Creek babbled its way through the valley, supporting grass and brush, beaver and fish, cattle and home-steaders.

'Headed straight up the valley, looks like,' Grant offered.

Carver nodded. 'Not fer long, likely,' he responded. 'Right around that first bend I 'spect the trail'll head up inta the hills.'

'Count on it, if it was that wild thing that stole 'im,' Grant agreed. 'You watch yourself, if you go follerin' the trail. You are fixin' to follow 'em, ain't ya?'

Carver smiled. 'That's my job. An' thanks. I'll watch myself.'

He nudged his horse into motion, riding about ten feet beside the trail he followed. He shifted in the saddle, trying to ease the knot that had returned to his gut. He brushed at the back of his neck, grum-bling at the tingling that persisted there. Get a grip on yourself, ya idiot! he scolded himself. Yer gettin' plumb spooky. Ghosts don't need horses ta ride.

As he expected, the trail indicated that the horse had run headlong for less than a mile. As the trail led past a point of land jutting into the valley, it was reined abruptly toward a narrow defile. The maw of that gully reached back into the mountain like the dark mouth of some dragon. Carver shuddered as he urged his horse into its opening.

The mouth of the draw was choked with brush. The tracks led into it as if following some invisible road. Carver loosened his Colt in its holster. He kept his hand on the gun's butt. He nudged the horse forward again, pushing through the brush.

More easily than he expected, horse and rider pushed through the brushy barrier. Beyond the tangled thicket, the bottom of the draw was flat and smooth. The tracks of the horse he trailed led straight up that path, worn smooth by the water from countless rains and snow-melts.

Carver glanced up at the sides of the draw, towering above him. They seemed to close in above him, penning him in, engulfing him. Sensations of being swallowed by the mountain gripped him. He shook his head against the feelings.

His horse gave no indication anyone was near. Trusting the animal's senses, he lifted the reins and followed the trail. It led half a mile into the mountain, following the gentle rise of the draw's floor. Then the tracks stopped.

He reined in, studying the ground. It took only moments. To his left, a clutter of shale and small rocks formed a rocky slope leading upward. It was too steep for his horse to climb with him aboard. As he dismounted he saw the tell-tale scuffs on rocks that marked the other horse's passing. He neither expected nor saw any human footprints. Even in his heavy boots, he didn't leave any mark on the rocks as he led the horse forward.

He scrambled, slipping and sliding on the loose and rolling stones, as he fought his way upward. After fifty yards, he reached the top of a narrow ridge. The rock slide gave way to solid ground. Carver eyed the ridge top that lay before him. Its narrow, almost barren top quickly broadened. As it did, the clear, grassy top gave way to brush, then to a thick stand of timber. It was impossible to see more than a dozen yards into the trees. Being so totally exposed on the top of the ridge made him tingle with more gut-wrenching warnings of imminent danger.

Moving quickly, he led his horse into the cover of the trees. He could see the tracks of the fleeing horse, still leading away through the trees. Can't be ridin' it in these trees, he reasoned, an' not a trace of a footprint. Gotta be an Indian er thet wild girl.'

Or something not human, the whisper in his mind suggested.

Walking carefully he began following the trail. He moved slowly. His eyes darted everywhere. Every step planted his foot softly and soundlessly. Either the fleeing horse-thief expected no pursuit or had planned for it. No attempt had been made to hide the horse's tracks.

He knew he was in imminent danger. He knew there would be a trap. Even so, he almost missed it. His foot stepped forward. Something felt wrong under the foot. Through the thick sole of his boot, he couldn't possibly have felt anything. But he felt something.

His eyes darted around again. Small birds flitted among the branches of the trees. A gray squirrel scuttled along a branch and disappeared behind a tree-trunk. A camp-robber jay scolded him for intruding. His eyes swept the ground before him. Nothing seemed out of place at all.

He frowned. Something wasn't right. He couldn't see it. He couldn't hear it. He couldn't really sense it at all. Still, he trusted the feeling.

He backed up a step, moving carefully. He picked up a broken tree-branch, lying where some sudden gust of wind had brought it down. He reached its four-foot length out in front of him. He began tapping the leaves and pine needles that carpeted the ground.

He walked forward carefully, tapping the ground in front of him in an arc before making each step. As his stick probed the spot on which his foot had been about to descend, something beneath the debris on the forest floor moved. A bowed tree, hidden behind a taller tree, snapped erect. Instantly a loop of rawhide leaped from beneath the needles. It caught the stick, jerking it out of his hand. It stopped, its lower end four feet above the ground, dangling in front of him.

Carver's gun was in his hand, as if of its own will. Following the movement of his eyes, the gun swept back and forth. Apart from the startled flight of half a dozen birds, nothing moved.

He took a deep breath. He holstered his gun.

'Pertneart got me,' he muttered. 'Thet was good!

I looked an' looked, an' I couldn't see nothin' atall what looked like it'd been disturbed. Either a Indian er thet wild thing all right, sure's anythin'.'

He found another stick and began tapping the ground in front of him as he moved forward. 'Not likely to try the same thing twice,' he scolded himself. Nonetheless, he continued to probe every step before he placed a foot.

After 200 yards the stand of timber stopped as quickly as it had begun. A narrow path snaked along the bottom of a steep slope. Too steep to climb, the slope still wasn't a sheer cliff. Only the old deer trail provided a way past it. Carver nodded at the faint traces of the horse's passing.

'Workin' on coverin' 'er tracks now,' he whispered. 'Doin' a right good job of it, too.'

He glanced up at the top of the slope. The rocky summit, framed against the impossible deep blue of the sky revealed no movement.

'Well, Scamp, let's see if we can stay on 'er trail,' he mumbled to his horse.

Stepping carefully, leading his horse, he began to follow the narrow trail. It led out around a shoulder of the slope, and he could not see it beyond that point. When he reached the bend, he leaned outward and looked around the protruding rocks, then jerked back quickly. He closed his eyes and digested the image that that quick look afforded. The trail stretched onward along the face of the slope. Nothing seemed out of the ordinary.

He leaned outward again, taking a longer look.

Nothing alarmed his senses. His eyes swept the slope, all the way to its top. Then he gazed in a careful circle, eyeing the slope below as well as above. He looked back over his horse at his back trail.

He stepped forward, leading the horse around the shoulder where the trail narrowed dangerously. The animal's ears went back. He eyed the ground nervously. He snorted softly. With mincing steps he tiptoed past the narrow spot, then took two quick steps on to the wider path, almost running into Carver.

Ignoring the animal's fear, Carver walked forward swiftly. The trail stretched straight ahead for fully a hundred yards before it disappeared in a clutter of brush and trees.

Half-way across that hundred yards he caught a movement in one of the ceaseless sweeps of his eyes, back and forth, up the slope and down. At the summit, he was sure he saw a movement. He stopped instantly, backing against his horse.

A large boulder dislodged from just below the summit, began to roll down the slope. He started pushing frantically against his horse. He pulled the reins back to the gelding's chest, forcing his head down and back. He talked urgently to the animal. 'Back up, boy! Back up! Back! Back!'

The horse tossed his head and snorted. He knew the trail was narrow. He could not see it at all behind him. A deep terror of unseen peril rose within him. His ears were laid back. His eyes rolled. But his master said to back up. A groan of fear wheezed through his nose, but he backed up. He backed up in halting, jerky steps, but he backed.

The boulder careened down the steep slope. As it bounced and bounded, it dislodged countless others of its kind. Buoyed by the company of its fellows, it began a frolicking dance that grew in size and speed with every yard. By the time it reached the narrow trail, it was an avalanche fifty yards wide. Hundreds of tons of rocks bounced and roared past the spot where Carver and his horse should have been.

Backed against the shoulder of the mountain where the path was too narrow to hope to back his horse, Carver watched with wide-eyed terror. Even when the rocky storm passed by, rattling and roaring on down the slope, he stood stock-still. After several minutes he swallowed hard. He passed a hand across the front of his trousers to reassure himself they were dry. Then he chuckled suddenly at his fear.

'Well, thet's twice she pertneart got me,' he said.

He scanned the top ridge of the slope carefully. Nothing moved. There was no sign of anyone's presence. 'Wonder if she watched long enough to know she didn't get me,' he pondered aloud.

The horse continued to toss his head, blowing nervously. Carver took a deep breath. 'Well, fella, let's try it again,' he ventured.

The horse was even more reluctant than before to follow this crazy master of his in paths of peril, but his loyalty and training remained stronger than his fear. They crossed the stretch of exposed path without incident.

Now Carver had to work to find the trail. It was there. He just had to move agonizingly slowly. He had to trust slight marks and disturbed twigs and blades of grass – signs that were so slight when he studied them carefully he couldn't be sure they were there. Yet, when his eye swept across them, something registered as an indicator, and he trusted those well-honed instincts.

The trail led up across the ridge and down into the next valley. It led always toward the taller mountains. It led down into a broad, flat bottom, with tiny springs in a hundred places. The trickle of water from the springs eventually joined together, forming a small creek that tumbled along toward its rendezvous with others of its kind. Together, they would become the north fork of Wind River, but that was a long way down the mountain.

As light began to fade, Carver sought a campsite. He chose a broad grassy area backed up against a sheer granite cliff that rose a hundred feet into the sky. A small spring gurgled up from the base of the cliff. Beyond the circle of grass, brush formed an almost perfect barrier against anyone's silent approach. Anyone moving through the brush in the darkness couldn't help making enough noise to alert either him or his horse.

Just to be sure, though, he used his lariat to picket the horse, tying him by a front leg. Within the circle of that rope, he could reach all the grass and water he might need.

Making a handful of fire with dry, smokeless wood,

Carver fixed himself some supper and a pot of coffee. When both were done, he carefully put out the fire, then rolled in his blankets. He was almost instantly asleep.

He had no idea what woke him. The moon was up. Its soft light flooded the earth with a deceptive sense of peace and security.

Trusting his instincts completely, he rolled from his blankets, gun in hand. Crouching against the granite cliff, he called softly: 'Who's there?'

No sound responded. Nothing moved.

Carver's eyes slowly swept the encircling brush, probing every shadow, seeking some sound, some movement. He could see nothing.

He looked at his horse. The gelding cropped grass, eating as if without a care in the world. Carver looked around at the brush again. Then his eyes darted back to the horse. It was in the wrong spot! The lariat wouldn't have let it move that close to the brush.

Moving swiftly and silently, he walked to the animal. Intent on filling his belly, the horse all but ignored him. Carver scratched his ears and patted his neck, keeping his eyes darting around the clearing. He ran a hand down the animal's leg. His fingers found the rope, tied in a loose bowline around the leg, just below the hock. It seemed tightly secured to the horse. He lifted the rope and pulled on it. It offered no resistance whatever.

Frowning, Carver looked down at the rope. Less than five feet from the horse, the rope had been

31

cleanly severed. He swore under his breath. Had that wild thing tried to steal his horse too? Had she just meant to release it, leaving him afoot? Where was she? How could she move through all that brush without making a sound? How could she disappear when he woke up, without even the horse being alarmed? Was he tracking a person, or some specter from a different world?

He swore at himself, forcing his thoughts into line. He used the horse's mane to lead him back to the end of the rope that was still secured. He knotted the severed ends of rope together. He walked back to his blankets. He picked up one blanket and sat down against the face of the cliff. He wrapped the blanket around himself and sat there, watching his horse, listening for any encroaching steps, for the remainder of the night.

He dozed from time to time. Each time he woke with a start, gun in hand. There was never anything he could see or hear that had wakened him.

With daylight he built his handful of fire again and started to fix himself some breakfast. He reached into the saddle-bag where his food was packed. He jerked the bag open and peered inside. It was empty. His bacon, hardtack, and jerky were gone.

Incredulous, he stared around again. Nothing moved. Swearing, he made a pot of coffee, settling for that, out of necessity, for breakfast. Then he mounted and set out to follow the trail.

By noon he gave up. The trail simply disappeared. It was as if the horse learned from its thief how to walk without disturbing so much as a blade of grass.

That night when he rode into Dubois it was nearly midnight. Nobody was on the street to greet him. Nobody was awake to ask him any questions. It was just as well. He was not in a good mood.

His mood was so foul he was almost too angry to notice that crawling sensation up his spine.

Almost.

The voice from the shadows brought it back instantly.

CHAPTER 4

'Marshal.'

The word reached softly from the shadows. Carver's reaction was anything but soft. Hunger that was gnawing a hole in his gut disappeared. Fatigue sloughed off like dirt in a downpour. He exploded from the saddle in a long dive. Hitting the ground with his shoulder tucked, he rolled in one continuous motion to his feet. His gun was in his hand. His horse was between him and the voice. From between the pommel of the saddle and the horse's neck he peered into the shadows.

'Who's there? Show yerself er I'll start shootin'!'

The voice responded at once. 'Don't shoot, Marshal! It's Phil. Phil Schwendmemamme... Oh, dang it, Marshal, you got me so spooked I can't even say my own name! Don't shoot me.'

Carver's stress and tension dissolved in a fit of laughter. He holstered his gun. Phil stepped into the street. Laughing so hard he could hardly stand, Carver walked around his horse's head. He pointed at Phil, trying to talk, but laughing too hard. 'Schwendmemamma did you say?'

'It ain't funny!' Phil protested, laughing in spite of himself.

'Funniest thing I ever heard in my life,' Carver argued. 'A man gets so spooked he cain't even say 'is own name! O' course, I ain't heard more'n three er four people could git the whole thing said when they wasn't spooked.'

'Schwendenhammer ain't that hard to say!' Phil insisted.

'It must be,' Carver cackled. 'You couldn't even say it yerself.'

'Well, dang it, Marshal, I thought you was gonna fill me plumb fulla holes afore I could even tell you who I was. Man, that was some stunt you pulled! You shot outa that saddle like a streak, then you was standin' up behind your horse a-pointin' your gun at me, an' I never even seen you hit the ground! How'd you do that? What are you so all-fired spooked about anyhow?'

Carver swiped at the tears rolling down his cheeks from laughing so hard.

'It's been a hard day,' he admitted. 'I been out-Injuned so bad it's pathetic. I ain't had nothin' to eat since yesterday. All the food got stole outa my pack. My best lariat got cut in two. I pertneart got caught in a rock avalanche. Then you popped up outa the shadows thataway! What'd you do that for anyhow?'

Even in the darkness Carver could see Phil's expression change.

'I been waitin' fer ya, since 'bout sundown. I sat down agin' the side o' your office, an' I guess I fell asleep. Heard your horse. Woke me up, so I just hollered at ya.'

'You been waitin' since sundown?'

'Yeah.'

'What's up?'

'You know Simon Blount?'

Carver frowned. He pushed up the back of his hat, scratching the back of his head.

'Blount. Blount. He that fella that homesteaded along East Fork, jist above where Bear Crick forks off?'

'That's him.'

'What happened to him?'

'He's dead.'

The subtle snake of foreboding crawled up Carver's back again.

'What from?'

'Got 'is throat cut.'

A gallon of sand settled in Carver's empty stomach.

'You find 'im?'

'Yeah.'

'Tell me about it.'

'Well, I was ridin' through there lookin' fer a bunch o' heifers we lost. I ride for the J–Bar, you know. Wayne, the straw boss, sent me down that way to see if I could pick up some sign of 'em. He worries about Putnam runnin' a long rope, so we look for our stuff down thataway ever' so often. I knowed Simon some. Rode with him on the U-Cross a couple years. Thought I'd stop in and say howdy, maybe have a bite to eat with 'im. Anyway, he was 'bout half way 'tween the house an' the crick. Had two buckets. Looked like he was carryin' 'em back from the crick. Dead on the ground. Gun in his hand. Lots o' blood all over the ground. Throat cut.'

'What'd ya do?'

'Up-chucked. Plumb puked my guts out is what I did, to be honest. Then I just sat down on the ground fer a while. Knees was wobblin' so bad they wouldn't hold me up. I seen men die afore. Some of 'em by gettin' throwed or stomped. Found one guy that froze to death. They never bothered me like that. Somethin' about the way . . . I dunno. I just sorta lost it.'

'Ya bury 'im?'

Phil shook his head. 'I didn't touch 'im no more, after I knowed he was dead. I figgered I'd oughta ride in here an' get you.'

Carver nodded. 'I'll ride out with you first thing in the morning. I'm too shot to head out tonight. I gotta get somethin' to eat an' get some sleep. Ya'd just as well come stay with me. I got an extra bedroom. We'll ride out at first light.'

Daylight found the pair in the saddle. The brisk trot at which they rode found them approaching Blount's homestead ahead of noon. The house was little more than a shack. It was dug back into the side of a hill, so the back wall was only about three feet high. Only the front wall was full height. It was built of an odd collection of logs, boards and hides. A buffalo hide served as a door.

'Not the tightest-built house I ever saw,' Carver observed.

Phil shook his head. 'Si wasn't never no hand fer looks er comfort,' he agreed. 'Took plumb good care of 'is stock, though. Good hand with cows er horses either. Good man with a gun, too. He could outdraw an' outshoot every man on the U–Cross.'

'That's goin' some,' Carver conceded. 'They got some hands that's more gunhand than cowboy.'

Phil nodded. 'Most folks figgered that's what Si was, too. He wasn't, though. Never knowed 'im to draw on anyone. He was jist naturally good.'

'Not good enough, apparently,' Carver observed.

Following the line of the lawman's sight, Phil saw a flock of crows and magpies, squabbling over the dead body stretched on the ground. Cursing, Phil jerked his rifle from the saddle scabbard. He levered a shell into the chamber. Carver's calm voice stopped him.

'Don't go shootin' up the place,' he said. 'They'll take off when we ride over there. You go chewin' up the ground with bullets, you might mess up whatever sign's there.'

Reluctantly Phil lowered the hammer on the rifle. He slid it back into its scabbard. Then he spurred his horse toward the dead man. Riding in a wide circle around the body, yelling at the top of his voice, he scattered the birds away from the body of his friend.

Then he slid from the saddle and gave up his breakfast to the hungry grass.

Carver dismounted and walked a slow circle
around the corpse.

'Buckets are both full o' water,' he observed aloud.
'He either set 'em down to talk to someone, or
dropped 'em an' they didn't upset.'

The body was face up, but the legs were tangled in
an awkward position. His right hand still held a Navy
Colt. A circle of blood stained the ground from a
point in line with the house, around the body to its
left. The circle of blood drew closer to the body as it
went, ending in a pool of blood that covered his
shoulder and chest.

Carver walked back and forth for nearly half an
hour, trying to find footprints. He could follow the
young man's tracks from the cabin to the creek, then
back again to where he lay. He could find no other
tracks.

Phil recovered from the latest attack of nausea,
and stood, white-faced and silent, watching the
lawman. At last he said: 'What d'ya make out,
Marshal?'

Without responding, Carver moved to the body.
He removed the gun from stiff fingers. He checked
the cylinder. He smelled the gun barrel. Then he
stood and surveyed the area.

When he was ready, he faced the shaken cowboy.

'Someone was layin' fer 'im,' he said. 'Most likely
hid in them bushes, down by the crick, though
there ain't a sign of any kind. When Blount filled 'is

buckets an' headed back to the house, he come up behind 'im. Probably grabbed his hair, an' slit 'is throat. He'da knocked his hat off, doin' that. That's how come the hat's layin' over there. Blount was a tough one, though. With his head cut 'most off, he dropped the buckets, drew his gun, turned around, an' got off one shot. Didn't likely hit nothin', but he got off a shot. He was sprayin' blood out somethin' fierce, an' dyin' so quick he couldn't get his feet turned around, so they got all tangled up. I 'spect he was dead when he hit the ground. Can't imagine a man bein' tough enough to turn around an' get off a shot after he gets 'is throat cut!'

'So who cut his throat?' Phil demanded.

'Well, it wasn't you,' Carver responded.

'Well, o' course it wasn't me! But how do you know?'

'You couldn't've done it without leavin' footprints. Whoever done it was plumb good at doin' it, too. He's done it afore.'

'But you don't have no idea who it is.'

'No, I don't. I'm just sure it wasn't you. I'm just as sure it wasn't one other person, too, but I cain't prove that as easy.'

'Who's that?'

'Doesn't matter.'

'You think it was that wild thing? You know, that half-animal, half-woman that's runnin' 'round the hills?'

Carver's lips compressed to a thin line.

'No, I'm plumb sure it wasn't her. Fer more reasons than one. I cain't prove it, though. Not yet.'

Maybe not ever, a voice in his head taunted.

CHAPTER 5

'Pardon me.'

Carver Dilling looked up from the papers on his battered desk.

'Can I help you?'

'Uh, yes. Well, perhaps. At least we hope so.'

Carver's eyes took in the well-tailored broadcloth suit, the neatly knotted tie, the expensive boots. The man was maybe fifty. Maybe less. Not much more, for sure. The woman who stepped into the office behind him looked closer to forty. Pretty. Well dressed. With no self-consciousness she folded the parasol that had protected her from the burning rays of the Wyoming sun.

The man cleared his throat.

'Uh, my name is Ralph Wadsworth. This is my wife, Dorothy.'

Carver swept off his hat, rose and stepped around the desk. He extended a hand.

'Glad to meet you,' he said, shaking a hand of each. Dorothy's handshake surprised him. He had sized them up as city folks, but her handshake betrayed an iron grip. 'How can I help you folks?'

'We, uh, well, we're looking for my niece. We've heard some rumors. We've got a lot of people who are listening and watching for us, and, well, we got a telegram from one of them.'

'Your niece?'

'Yes. Her name is Kylee Wadsworth.'

Carver shook his head. 'Never heard the name.'

'Uh, no. I was sure you hadn't. May we tell you our story?'

'Sure. Of course. Uh, sit down, won't ya?'

He waved at a couple chairs against the wall. They both sat down, watching him carefully. At a loss, he retreated behind the cover of his desk and sat down.

'Go ahead an' spit it out,' he said.

The man took a deep breath and began.

'We are from Nebraska. We have a rather substantial farm there. Most of our family live in that region. It's an area that's been good to us. But my brother, Kyle, and his wife – her name was Lea – they wanted to go further west. I'm afraid they were the adventurous ones in the family . . .'

'Especially Lea,' Dorothy interjected. 'She could outride and outshoot and outwork most men. She was always looking for something new and exciting to try.'

'I'm afraid her nature was a strong influence on my brother,' Ralph agreed. 'On the other hand, it was exactly that quality in her that attracted him, I think. They were well suited to each other.'

Dorothy sighed heavily. 'I can't deny that. They were well matched.'

Carver swallowed his impatience, waiting for them to get on with the story. After what seemed a long time, Ralph continued:

'Well, anyway, that's not really part of the story. The fact is, they sold out the farm they had. They came West. They homesteaded on Fifteen Mile Creek.'

'Up north-west of Worland?' Carver interrupted.

They both nodded at once. Ralph continued:

'They had a very nice homestead there. Shipped in milled lumber for their house. Real glass in the windows. Very good land, I think. More suited for cattle than farming, I think, but they both leaned more to ranching than farming anyway. Cattle and horses both, they wanted to raise.'

'Arabians,' Dorothy interrupted again. 'They had some very good blood-lines to start a herd. I'm sure their horses would have become among the best in the state.'

'Yes, well, anyway,' Ralph took over the narrative again, 'it seems that a marauding band of Indians descended on them, for no real reason we've been able to ascertain. They put up a creditable struggle, but, in the end, were overwhelmed. They were killed.'

'They have kids?' Carver asked.

Again, the couple nodded as if one.

'They had three,' Dorothy said softly. 'Kylee was fourteen. Randall was twelve. Sophia was eight.'

'They killed the kids too?' Carver asked.

Dorothy's head dropped, and her eyes lowered enough so that Carver could not see them. Ralph's eyes grew suspiciously moist.

'Two of them,' he confirmed. 'Kyle and Lea, Randall and Sophia, were all found in the yard. They'd been, well, rather viciously mutilated. Terribly mutilated, in fact. Even the little girl, Sophia, appeared to have been, uh, very brutally used before she was killed.'

'But not the other one? What was her name?'

'Kylee,' Ralph offered. 'She was fourteen. No trace of her was found. It was assumed that the Indians took her as a captive. We sent extensive enquiries through a number of people. Marshals. Mountain men. The army. Everyone we could find. We hired three different men to try to find out what happened to her. She was never offered, as captives sometimes are, I guess, for ransom. Nobody has found her. It was rumored, though, and we heard the rumor from two of the three men we hired, that it was a band of Crow Indians that had captured her, and that one of them had taken a fancy to her, and kept her for his own, uh, well, wife, I suppose.'

'I remember the incident,' Carver confirmed. 'It was about four years ago. Maybe five. Band o' Crows went on the warpath. Killed a bunch o' folks, afore gettin' chased back up on the Yellowstone somewheres.'

'That would have been the time,' Dorothy agreed. 'It was almost five years ago.'

'That'd make her 'bout nineteen now, if she's still alive,' Carver said.

They both nodded again. 'Her birthday was just about a month ago,' Dorothy agreed. 'She would have turned nineteen.'

'So what's this have to do with me?' Carver asked.

Ralph cleared his throat. 'Well, our sources . . . Mind you, we've kept some feelers out, all this time, hoping that some time we'd hear something. And, from time to time, we've heard things, but nothing we could confirm.'

Dorothy interrupted again. 'We heard once that she had a baby, by the savage that kidnapped her, but we were never able to confirm that.'

Ralph took control of the conversation again. 'More recently, we heard a rumor that she had escaped the tribe. That she had lost her mind. That she was living in the mountains like an animal, and even the Indians were afraid of her. Or couldn't find her. Most recently, we have heard rumors . . . well, more accurately, information we have paid for, indicates a girl of that description has been seen in this vicinity. On the outside chance the rumors may be true, and that it just might be her, we have come to see if you know anything.'

'What would this girl look like?'

'She would be nineteen years old,' Dorothy repeated. 'She was always slender-built, very athletic, like her mother. Very dark hair. Black, even. If she favors her mother as much as she seemed to as a younger girl, she would be uncommonly strong and very bright. I'm afraid that's the best description we can give you.'

Carver pondered the information for a long while in silence. At last he spoke.

'Well, there's a rumor – well, it's more than a rumor, I guess – there's a girl out there somewhere in the hills that sorta fits that description. Folks been callin' 'er "the Wild Thing". Some folks argue she's really a animal. Or part-animal, part-human – you know how stories are when they get goin'. There was a young homesteader up north who was rumored to be talkin' to 'er. Got 'er to trust 'im some. Feedin' 'er, an all. Nobody's ever heard 'er talk, but one o' the guy's friends thought she understood all right enough.'

'You don't say!' Ralph enthused. 'Where is this homesteader? We must go speak with him at once.'

'I'm afraid that ain't gonna be possible.' Carver dashed their hopes. 'He went an' got himself killed.'

'Killed? How?'

'Somebody slit 'is throat, sittin' at his kitchen table.'

Dorothy made a small choked sound and covered her mouth with her hands.

'What? By whom?' asked Ralph.

Carver shrugged. 'Don't know. Most folks assume it was the Wild Thing. The guy's best friend figgers he got 'er tamed down enough to think that he could, uh, make advances, an' she cut 'is throat. 'Bout the same time, someone stole a horse from the next place up the crick. I follered the horse, an' I'm pertneart sure it was her stole the horse. I pertneart got myself kilt twice tryin' to track 'er, then I lost the trail.'

The couple were lost in silence for a long moment. A choked sound, like a muffled sob, broke through Dorothy's clenched hands in front of her mouth. Eventually Ralph spoke.

'Do you think she did it?'

Carver studied them carefully before he answered. Then he said:

'Well, I got no proof, either way. But I'll tell ya somethin' I ain't told nobody else. In my own mind, I'm plumb sure she didn't do it.'

Two pairs of eyes fixed intently on his face.

'Why do you say that?' Dorothy breathed softly.

'Well, whilst I was up in the hills, hot on 'er trail, tryin' my best to catch up with 'er, another home-steader was killed the same way. I know good an' well the second one wasn't her, 'cause I'm sure I wasn't that fur behind her two valleys over. She couldn'ta been in both places at once.'

The couple pondered the information for a long moment. 'So, may I assume that you have some plan?' asked Ralph. 'That you do intend to do some-thing?'

Carver admitted as much. 'I been thinkin'. It seems to me I got two different problems here. One is a wild girl what's scared of ever'thin' and ever'-body. She sure needs help from someone. The other is a couple murders that it's my job to solve. It seems to me my best bet is to find the girl, then find out

WILD THING

what she knows about the killin's.'

'And how do you purpose to do that?'

'I ain't real sure. But if she is that niece o' yours, that'll help. It'd help if I had her real name to call 'er, if I kin git close enough for 'er to hear it. So maybe I'll start by driftin' up among the Crows for a short spell, an' see if it's her, an' she got away from 'em.'

'You can do that?'

'I kin try.'

'Can you speak with them?'

'Nope. But I know a Shoshoni named Lean Wolf. He kin. I'll take 'im along.'

Another long silence ensued.

'Well! When may we expect to hear something from you?'

'Cain't answer thet. Ya write down where an' how to wire ya, an' I'll send a wire soon's I know somethin', either way.'

'Oh, we do really appreciate that,' Dorothy assured him. 'It's been such a long and heartbreaking time. To have even this small chance, after all these years, is almost too much to hope for.'

'Well,' Carver cautioned, 'don't go gettin' yer hopes too high. If it's her, she's likely been hardused. Mostly, if young girls ain't got back from the Indians in the first three months er so, they ain't never right again, even if they is found. It's been pertneart five years.'

Dorothy looked like she was about to cry again. Ralph's lips were drawn into a thin line.

'We are aware of that reality,' he said. 'We have discussed that possibility. However, it is our duty to try our best, and, at the very least, to see to it that she is well and compassionately cared for, if she remains alive.'

'I'll see what I kin do,' Carver assured them.

That knot in his gut came again. He sat down abruptly as the Wadsworths walked out the door.

CHAPTER 6

'Not like Crow.'

Lean Wolf's voice was flat, almost totally devoid of expression.

'They ain't my favorite folks neither,' Carver admitted.

'Girl gone,' Lean Wolf asserted for probably the fourth time. 'No need go there.'

'Maybe not,' Carver conceded. 'But I gotta. An' I need an interpreter. It's purty hard to be sure I know what I'm seein' in sign language. You speak Crow.'

'Not like Crow,' Lean Wolf repeated.

'Twenty dollars,' Carver replied.

Lean Wolf's eyes darted to his, then away. He looked off across country for a long moment. He licked his lips.

'Gold?'

'Gold.'

'One talk?'

'One talk.'

'You bring army?'

'No. I don't 'spect the army'd be interested in sendin' an escort for this. It'll just be me'n you.'

'Not like Crow.'

'Twenty dollars. Gold. One week. Two weeks at the most.'

'Take Two Knives.'

'He don't like the Crow neither. I ain't sure they'd talk to him either.'

'Take Two Knives with you and me. We maybe get to leave alive if Two Knives there too. They have big fear of Two Knives.'

Carver considered the request. Two Knives was the Shoshone name for Johnny Rasmussen. He had been a captive of the Crow for several months as a youth. His family had been killed. When he escaped, the stories said he had attacked four Crow warriors, wielding a knife in each hand, killed all four, and left. For some reason the Crow were afraid to pursue him.

He worked around on various ranches, but remained always reclusive and quiet. He was one of the few men Carver had ever known who wore two guns, and he always wore two knives as well. One of the guns was in a holster on his hip. The other was high up on the other side, butt forward. The two knives were always at his belt. It was rumored that he could draw and throw both knives at the same time, then draw and empty one of the pistols before the knives reached their target. Even though the rumors were doubtless exaggerated, Carver knew there was a deep and abiding fear of him among the Crows. Having him along would either ensure their being allowed to leave safely, or it would ensure their being killed out of hand.

'I will talk with Two Knives.'

'I wait here two suns.'

Carver nodded and rose to leave. It took him half a day to locate Johnny Rasmussen. He was working for the D–Slash outfit, and was high up in the mountains checking out a batch of cows and calves.

'You know about the Wild Thing?' Carver asked, when he eventually located him.

'Heard of 'er,' Johnny replied.

'Did you know her, when you was with the Crows?'

Johnny shook his head without answering.

'Was she with the same bunch o' Crows?'

Again he shook his head in silence.

'Well, do you know what village, or what bunch, she was with?'

He nodded.

'Who owned 'er?'

'Fast Dog.'

Carver knew his breath must have caught in his throat, but he did not let on.

'Do you know where his village is?'

Johnny thought in silence for several minutes.

'Maybe.'

'Between you an' Lean Wolf, ya reckon you could find it?'

A cloud crossed the young man's eyes, but his face betrayed no expression.

'Why.'

Carver sighed. He wasn't used to having to justify his

actions or his decisions. It niggled him. Yet he needed the young man, with his fearsome reputation among the Crows. If the reason didn't seem adequate, he knew the lad would turn and ride away without even bothering to answer him. He decided his only chance of securing an ally was in being open and honest.

'They's been a couple men murdered. Both of 'em had their throats slit. One of 'em, Will Tanning, was tryin' to coax out the Wild Thing. He was feedin' 'er. Talkin' to 'er, I guess. He ended up with 'is throat cut. The Wild Thing – at least I figger it was her – stole a horse from Grant Tucker. Lit out. I trailed 'er. Pertneart got myself killed. Lost 'er trail. Then Simon Blount got killed. Same way. Throat cut. Only he got killed whilst I was gallivantin' around up in the mountains, chasin' after thet Wild Thing. So I'm sure she ain't the one done it. But she's gettin' blamed, nohow.'

'Fast Dog.'

'What about Fast Dog?'

'He killed 'em.'

'Fast Dog did? How do ya know that?'

Johnny shrugged. 'His woman got away. Escaped. Like me. Only she didn't kill the ones guardin' 'er. Didn't do nothin' to make 'em scared of 'er. She jist got away. He's mad. Tryin' to find 'er. He's killin' anyone he thinks is helpin' 'er.'

The speech was the longest Carver had ever heard of the reclusive young man giving. He hesitated to quiz him, but felt he had to.

'Ya seen 'im?'

Johnny shook his head.

'Ya jist guessin'?'

Johnny nodded.

'Well, ya may be right. But me, I gotta find out. I gotta go talk to this Fast Dog.'

'He's a liar.'

'Ain't they all?'

Johnny shook his head vigorously.

'No. Most of 'em's honest, 'cept when it's OK to lie. Like to white men. Or tradin' horses or stuff. Or braggin' 'bout coup to other tribes, not their own. Or . . .'

'I git the picture,' Carver interrupted. 'I'm payin' twenty dollars gold to go with me'n Lean Wolf to palaver with Fast Dog.'

'Why me?'

' 'Cuz Lean Wolf won't go unless you do. He thinks the Crow is some scared o' ya. He thinks we might manage to ride out agin, with our scalps still on our heads, if you're along.'

'If I see one I don't like, kin I kill 'im?'

Carver shook his head. 'Not unless we gotta fight our way out. I'm a lawman. I gotta go by the law.'

'They ain't white folks.'

'Yeah, I know. But the law's the same.'

'Not to them.'

'It is to me. Twenty dollars. Back my hand. No killin' unless we gotta. Thet's the deal.'

Johnny squatted on the ground. He picked up a stick and doodled in the dirt for several minutes. Then he stood.

'I'll do it. When?'

'Now.'

'You tell Walt?'

'I told 'im. He's sendin' another hand up to take over here fer ya.'

Without another word, Johnny jumped on his horse, without using the stirrup. He wheeled and trotted off, with Carver close behind.

Three days later the young man had still not spoken another word. They had ridden into the village where Lean Wolf waited. They simply sat their horses. Lean Wolf stepped out of his tepee, nodded, and went back inside. When he emerged he was ready to go. He caught his horse, loaded what few things he needed, and mounted. Johnny rode out, leading the way. Carver followed. Lean Wolf brought up the rear.

Two nights they camped. Each assumed a share of the duties in camp. There was no conversation. None of the three spoke.

The third day they sat together on a hill overlooking a Crow village along the Yellowstone River.

'Thet the right one?' Carver asked.

Rather than answer, Johnny merely shrugged. They rode directly to the village. Though their arrival appeared to cause little stir within the village, Carver noticed several Indians in strategic locations. When they entered the village they would be surrounded.

Before they did, Johnny reined his horse to the side. While he was still where he could not be encircled, he said: 'I'll wait here.'

Recognizing at once the wisdom of the young man's strategy, Carver nodded. He and Lean Wolf continued to the center of the village.

They were studiously ignored. They stopped in an open space and sat their horses in silence, as courtesy demanded. After a quarter of an hour, an old Indian came out of his tepee. He spoke in Crow.

'He says "Welcome to two who come in peace".' said Lean Wolf. 'He say Two Knives not welcome.'

'Tell 'im Two Knives waits for us outside the camp.'

Lean Wolf said something. The old Indian looked at the feared young man, sitting his horse well within pistol-shot. He was clearly uncomfortable.

'I notice he ain't asked us to git down,' Carver observed.

'He not do that,' Lean Wolf agreed. ' "Welcome" not mean "welcome". It only mean they not kill us yet.'

'Well, thet's real comfortin' to know. Tell 'im I wanta talk with Fast Dog.'

'It is pretty quick to say your business. We have not talked much yet.'

'Yeah, I know, but the skin's crawlin' up my back somethin' awful. I got a feelin' there's about ten arrows an' six er eight guns pointed at us.'

'You expected willow switches?' Lean Wolf responded. 'I will ask.'

He spoke again in Crow. He spoke for a long while. When he fell silent, Carver spoke.

'That was a powerful lot o' talkin' for what you needed to say.'

'There are customs. I had to admire the village and the chief. I had to tell him how beautiful the women of this village are.'

'But we ain't seen none of 'em.'

'Don't matter none. I told him how much people talk of this village of the Crow, an' how they are known for being very brave, and for being men of their word. I told 'im we had heard much of Fast Dog, and wished to meet a great warrior of the Crow.'

'Any o' thet true?'

'Don't matter none.'

The old Indian spoke for quite as long as Lean Wolf had spoken.

'Must be the day for makin' speeches,' Carver observed.

'It is always a time to make speeches when visitors arrive,' Lean Wolf agreed. 'He still not happy about Two Knives covering our backsides. He does not have the upper hand he likes always to have. But he will call for Fast Dog.'

'But he still ain't asked us to git down.'

'That is not a bad thing. I like to have a fast horse between my legs when I am in a Crow village.'

'Yeah, thet ain't a bad idea, all right.'

The old Indian turned and said something over his shoulder. Instantly a young squaw emerged from his tepee and hurried across the village. Outside another tepee she stopped and spoke.

At once the flap of that tepee was tossed back. A muscular Indian emerged and straightened in the sun. Even from that distance, Carver could see a large scar across his face.

'That Fast Dog?' he asked softly.

'That is Fast Dog.'

'He looks plenty salty. Where'd 'e git the scar?'

'From the fast dog. When he was born, one of the dogs was hungry. It tried to take a bite out of his face. It was so fast the woman who was helping with the birth could not knock it away before it bit him.'

'So he was named fer the dog what bit 'im.'

'It is better than Dead Dog, I think, which is what the dog was very quickly. It was the next meal of his mother.'

The scarred warrior approached and stopped beside the old man. He spoke in Crow.

'He say he is Fast Dog,' Lean Wolf translated. 'Wants to know who has heard of him among the white men.'

'Well, tell 'im however ya need to. Then ask whether he has a white wife.'

Fast Dog's eyes flickered as Carver said the words. He was instantly sure the Indian understood English, and made a note to be careful what he said. Lean Wolf made another long speech.

'Figgerin' he understands both, what'd you tell 'im?' Carver asked.

Lean Wolf's eyes darted to Fast Dog for just an instant before he answered.

'I told him about the way we have heard of his brave deeds and his many coup all the way to the Wind River. I told him we had heard he was a man who could satisfy many women, so he had many wives. I told him we had heard he even had a white wife who stayed with him because he is very much man.'

'Tell 'im we'd like to talk to his white wife. Someone wants to know if maybe she's related to 'em, an' that she's OK.'

Lean Wolf nodded, and spoke in Crow again.

Fast Dog did not answer for several minutes. As he waited, his jaw became visibly more tightly clamped. His eyes blazed as he answered.

'Don't seem too happy 'bout it,' Carver observed when he had finished.

Lean Wolf translated.

'He say he does indeed have a wife who is a white woman. He says they have a child, but the child has become dead. He say that someone has stolen his wife, because she would not leave him on her own, but he will find her. He says that he will hunt her until the snows grow deep if he has to, and he will find her. He has been hunting her, and knows where she was taken. Whoever has her, or touches her, he will kill. He say he has already killed many white men for her, and will kill many more if he must. He say he is a great warrior who has counted very many coup.'

Without waiting to be answered, Fast Dog spoke again. It was only a single sentence this time.

'He says if we wish to live, we will go now,' Lean Wolf said.

'Then I 'spect we'd best do that,' Carver observed.

'You go first. I watch your back,' Lean Wolf replied.

Without saying anything further, Carver lifted his reins and wheeled his horse. He rode slowly, trying his best to give the impression they had no fear. If he succeeded, he was a bigger liar than Fast Dog, he thought.

Lean Wolf rode close behind him. As they reached where Johnny waited, he muttered:

'Two of 'em slipped outa camp. They'll be layin' fer us. Look sharp.'

Carver and Lean Wolf kept their eyes busy. Their heads swivelled from side to side, trying to probe every bit of cover. They were more than a quarter of a mile from the village when Johnny stood suddenly in his stirrups. A knife appeared as if by magic in each hand. Both of them were loosed simultaneously, each into a clump of brush on either side of the trail.

Carver decided maybe the rumors were true. By the time the knives thunked into flesh and bone, followed by twin grunts, Johnny had a gun in each hand. He kicked his horse, and the animal lunged forward. Just past the bushes that stood on either side of the trail, he wheeled and came back toward them. He swerved from the trail, passing by the bush on one side. Keeping his horse in a dead run, he rode in a circle around the other bush. He leaped from the running steed and reached into the bush. He jerked out a Crow warrior by the hair. The man was dead. One of Johnny's knives protruded from his chest.

Lunging across the trail to the other bush, Johnny repeated his actions. The Crow who had crouched there, waiting, was just as dead. The haft of Johnny's second knife protruded from the base of his throat.

Carver swallowed hard.

'I hadn't even seen 'em. How'd you know they was there?'

Johnny didn't bother answering. He jerked the knife free of the Indian brave's throat. With swift strokes, he severed the man's head.

Carrying the head, he crossed back over the trail and did the same with the other one. Then he carefully cleaned both knives and replaced them in their sheaths. Carrying the head of one of the warriors in each hand, he leaped into the saddle and kicked his horse into motion.

Carver and Lean Wolf fell in behind him. Carver sure hoped Lean Wolf knew what was happening. He himself had no idea.

Three miles further they came to a deep ravine. Standing at the edge of the ravine, Johnny whirled a complete circle, using his spin as momentum to throw the head of one of the warriors as far as he could fling it out into the abyss. Then he did the same with the other. Then he mounted his horse and continued on his way, with the other two in tow.

'What'd 'e do thet fer?' Carver asked Lean Wolf over his shoulder.

'It is what he does,' Lean Wolf replied. 'It is the reason the Crow fear him so much. It is believed among the Crow that to do that means the warrior who was killed will never have a head in the next life, unless his wives can find it and bury it with him. He tries to see that they cannot do that. In that way, they think he can kill both their body and their soul. That is much worse than just getting killed.'

'Well, it works on me,' Carver shuddered. 'He's one fella I don't want mad at me.'

'Did you find out what was worth the forty dollars you paid us?' Lean Wolf asked. There was a distinct note of taunting in his voice.

'Guess I jist wasted forty dollars o' the gov'ment's money,' Carver lamented.

But it wasn't quite wasted. He had learned that the Wild Thing, if it was Fast Dog's runaway wife, had had a child, and the child was dead. He also had one more suspect for the two murders.

CHAPTER 7

'Dilling, I wanta know what you're doin' about them killin's.'

Carver looked up casually at the big rancher towering over his desk. Then, as if dismissing him, he returned to the papers he was working on. After a moment's pregnant silence, without looking up, he spoke.

'And you, I believe, are Vince Putnam. Is that correct?'

'You dang well know it is.'

'And if I ain't mistaken, you are the illustrious owner of the V–Bar–T ranch.'

'What're you tryin' to pull, Dilling? You blessed well know who I am an' where my ranch is.'

As if he had not been answered, Carver continued, leaning back in his chair.

'You know, Putnam . . .'

'Mr Putnam!' Putnam corrected.

'Oh! I'm sorry. I didn't know we were using social niceties today. To save me, I can't remember you calling me "Mr Dilling" when you came in, or "Marshal Dilling". I thought this must be a day to use last names only or something.'

A slightly built, swarthy hand, standing one step to the rancher's right, spoke up.

'The boss says his name is Mr Putnam. You call him Mr Putnam.'

Carver smiled as if in a conversation over coffee.

'And who might you be?'

'Me Charley. I work fer Mr Putnam.'

'Charley. Now would that be a last name also? Is your name something Charley, or is it Charley something?'

Charley's eyes flashed. His hand dropped down to hover over the butt of a Colt .45, tied low on his hip.

'You makin' fun of Charley?' he demanded.

Carver smiled broadly. 'Just askin'. You got any name other'n Charley?'

'Charley White,' Putnam interjected. 'You'd be well advised not to rile 'im.'

'My name is Charley White Man,' Charley corrected.

Carver nodded mentally. He had already noted the man's swarthy complexion, the high cheekbones, the straight black hair. He didn't know if he were mostly Indian with some white blood, or half and half. Sioux, he guessed.

Although he appeared to be relaxed, Carver had moved his legs back until his weight was balanced on the balls of his feet, so he could move off the chair quickly if he needed to. Out of sight of both men, he quietly gripped a short length of ax handle that leaned beside his chair. He addressed the rancher.

'Well, now that we have the introductions out of the way, why don't you two boys go back out in the street, knock on my door, walk in and ask "Marshal Dilling", or maybe, "Mr Dilling", if you may be given information concerning the murder investigations.'

Putnam's face turned such a deep red it was almost purple. A low growl seemed to force its way up from somewhere deep in his bowels.

Charley's response was quicker, and far more deadly. Without any change of expression, his hand swept up from his holster, gripping his Colt .45.

Just as his hand leveled, Carver, no longer in the chair, brought the length of ax-handle down hard on the half-breed's wrist. It cracked like two pieces of wood striking together. The gun dropped from his hand and clattered on to the desk.

Without seeming to stop, Carver swung the ax-handle in a loop that brought it sharply against the left side of Charley's head. He crumpled without a sound.

Putnam's face turned yet a shade deeper. His eyes bulged. Carver sat back down in his chair as if nothing had happened. He addressed the rancher.

'Like I said, you oughta drag this piece o' trash outa here, then come back in like you're talkin' ta an equal, if ya got questions ya want answered.'

Giving every appearance of ignoring the big rancher, Carver returned to working on the papers on his desk. He moved Charley's gun over to the end of the desk away from the rancher, making it appear as if he were simply moving it off his papers. As he did, he lowered the hammer, taking note that the man was extremely fast with his gun. Only Carver's own greater speed, and his having his moves planned in advance, had kept him from being a target. Dead target, he corrected.

After what seemed like several minutes, but was actually less than a minute, the rancher chuckled. He reached down and grabbed Charley by the collar and dragged him to the door as easily as if he were a child. He heaved him out the door, then turned and walked back to the desk.

'All right, Marshal Dilling, kin I ask about thet thar investigation now?'

Carver leaned back, smiling broadly. 'Ah, that sounds a whole lot better, Mr Putnam. What would you like to know?'

Putnam had now played the part as long as his chagrin would allow. His voice turned abruptly surly and demanding again.

'I wanta know if you're gettin' up a posse to go after thet Wild Thing.'

'Now why would I do thet?'

'Fer them murders! Why else?'

'Who said she committed those murders?'

'Oh, knock it off, Marshal! Everybody in the country knows she done it.'

'And how do they know thet?'

'Well, who else would it be?'

'Oh, it could be any number of people. You even.'

'Me? What in Sam Hill makes you say a dang fool thing like that? Why would it be me?'

'Well, there's a thing lawmen call "motive". It means that the first thing we ask, when someone gets killed, is "Who wanted this fella dead?" or "Who has somethin' ta gain from this fella gettin' killed?" An' from thet question, your name jist come up first off.'

'Why me?' Putnam repeated.

'Well, ya got a purty sizable spread up along East Fork. Got a lotta cows. More cows than ya got grass fer, as a matter o' fact. Use a lot o' gov'ment range.'

'So what? Every rancher does that.'

'True. But the more o' the land what gets home-steaded, the harder it gets fer ya to let your cows run on gov'ment range. They's less of it. They's other fella's cows on more of it. You're gettin' crowded, ain't ya, Mr Putnam?'

'Everybody's gettin' a little crowded,' Putnam conceded. 'So what?'

'Well, let me see if I got the lay o' the land right. Bear Crick, an' Wiggin's Fork, an' North Fork all flow inta East Fork, right?'

'So?'

'Then East Fork, it runs on fer quite a ways afore it spills inta Wind River. So from your place, if'n a fella jist follers up the crick, purty soon Bear Crick branches off, then North Fork branches off, then Wiggin's Fork branches off. If them homesteaders wasn't there along East Fork, your cows could foller them cricks an' graze clear up inta the mountains.'

'That's the way they used to do,' Putnam conceded.

As if he hadn't been interrupted, Carver continued: 'So ever' time one o' them homesteaders gits discouraged er somethin', ya got a standin' offer to buy out his homestead claim. Then ya put a hand on it ta finish provin' up on it, then ya aim to buy it offa him.'

'There's nothing against the law in that.'

'That's a fact. Nobody ever said they was. Unless somebody doesn't wanta sell to ya. Then what d'ya do, Mr Putnam?'

'What d'ya mean, what do I do? I wait till they are ready to sell.'

'But would ya have ta? What if something happened to somebody what didn't want to sell. Can you get a quitclaim deed to finish provin' up on that homestead?'

'O' course. You're a lawman. You know that.'

'So what I'm saying, Mr Putnam, is that you have more motive than anyone I know for wantin' them men dead an' off their homesteads.'

'Are you accusin' me o' murder?'

'Nope. You jist asked me who else besides thet Wild Thing mighta kilt them fellas. I was jist explainin' who mighta. Coulda been most anyone. Even you.'

'That ain't funny.'

Carver stood abruptly. 'I wasn't tryin' to be funny, Mr Putnam. But I am tryin' to be civil. Now I'll tell ya that I am doin' my job, and I'll keep on doin' my job, an' I'll find out who killed them fellas. An' I'll do it without you buttin' in an' askin' a whole bunch o' questions thet ain't none o' your business. Now if that's all you come in here fer, ya'd jist as well leave.'

The rancher's eyes bored angrily into him, but Carver returned the stare with every bit as much intensity. The growl he had heard before rumbled deep in the rancher's throat as he whirled and stomped out.

As he stepped out the door he nudged Charley, who was sitting up, holding the side of his head.

'Get your gun and come on,' he ordered. 'I'll be at the saloon.'

Charley struggled to his feet. He looked daggers at Carver as he stepped back into the office. He staggered sideways, then righted himself. One hand gripped the hilt of the knife at his belt, but he made no further threatening gesture.

'Kin I have my gun?' he asked.

Carver shrugged. He picked up the Colt and opened the cylinder. He dumped the shells out of it, then handed it to Charley.

'If ya ever pull it on me again, I'll bury it with ya,' he promised.

Charley opened his mouth to say something, then thought better of it. He holstered the gun and walked unsteadily out into the sunlight.

'I surprised 'im today,' Carver muttered softly. 'He won't surprise again. And thet's a very dangerous man.'

CHAPTER 8

'Howdy, Marshal.'

Carver looked the young man up and down. He was dressed in buckskins, and wore moccasins. His hair hung well below his shoulders. It had received scant attention for a long while. His beard was every bit as unkempt. Smells jist like the last bear I shot, Carver thought.

Aloud, he said, 'Mornin'. Ya waitin' fer me?'

'Yup. Figgered you'd be a-openin' up your office directly.'

'OK.'

Carver unlocked and opened the door to his small office and stepped aside. The young man entered. Carver motioned him to one of the chairs.

'So who are ya?' Carver asked, 'an what kin I do fer ya?'

'Name's Green. Casper Green,' the mountain man offered. 'Heard you was lookin' fer a girl.'

'A girl?'

'Wild un.'

'Yeah, matter o' fact I have been. Ain't been sure it was a girl, though.'

'She's a girl. Squats, anyhow.'

'You've seen 'er?'

He nodded. 'Onct. Then she caught my scent or heard me or somethin'. Lit out. 'Twas like she jist disappeared. Never seen nothin' like it. She was squattin' in the bushes. Her head come up like she heard somethin'. Then she jist warn't there no more. Never heard 'er move. Never seen a twig wobble. She jist all of a sudden wasn't there no more.'

'So you don't really know where she is.'

'Close. She ain't left the valley.'

'What valley's that?'

'You know Wiggin's Fork?'

'Some.'

'You know how it narrows plumb down, like it ain't goin' nowheres?'

'Uh huh.'

'Been past there?'

'Nope. Too narrow. 'Cept maybe late in the year, water's pretty fast. Pretty steep. Be real hard to get up it, even afoot.'

The mountain man nodded.

'Past that, way up high, it opens up again.'

'Another valley?'

He nodded. 'Right purty one. Good trappin'. Bad in the winter, though. No way out, once the snows pile up. Stuck in there till April. Maybe May.'

'You've wintered in there?'

'Nope. Trapped it early. Pelts git prime up there

early. Got out afore the big snows. They's been fellas winter in there afore, though.'

'You go in through the gorge?'

He shook his head. 'Too risky. Brung my furs out thataway, though. Floatin' down the crick's different than goin' in. They's another way in.'

'How's thet?'

The mountain man rose and walked out into the edge of the street. He drew a rough map in the dirt with his finger.

'If'n ya foller East Fork up here, eight er ten miles past Putnam's, then break off on North Fork five, six miles, they's a real little crick what comes in on your left. Foller it about a mile, till you see a spot right about here where you kin climb up toward the top. Deer trail there. They's two big ol' cottonwoods right afore ya git to it. Cain't miss it. Not hardly any cottonwoods up thet high. Foller thet deer trail up acrosst, then drop down in the next valley an' straight up t'other side. It's a long climb. Foller thet ridge ta your right 'bout three, four miles. They's three big tall rocks standin' side by side. Half a mile past 'em, you'll see a spot where a deer trail angles down toward the bottom. Foller it. You'll go down a ways, then back up agin. You'll top out over a ridge, an' the whole valley'll be laid out right in front o' ya. Ya kin foller thet deer trail all the way ta the bottom.'

'Sounds like a long way in.'

' 'Tis. Thet's why nobody goes in there. Pertneart nobody knows it's there.'

'How big a valley?'

73

'Oh, maybe ten, twelve miles long. Mile er two wide.'

'No kiddin'!'

'Purtiest sight ya'll ever see, when ya top out on thet last ridge. Reg'lar trees 'n brush goin' down toward the bottom. Bottom's kinda brushy. Patches o' open grass here'n there. Along the bottom they's big pines. Whoppin' big pines. Crick splits up inta three er four branches, then comes back together. Mountains up behind it is snow-capped all year. Couple ol' cabins, where fella's wintered in there. Ain't been used in half a dozen years, though.'

'And you say she's hidin' out in there?'

'She's there somewheres. Ya ain't likely to spot 'er, but she's there.'

'All right. Thanks. I'll ride up an' have a look.'

'You'd best not wait a lot.'

'Why's that?'

'It's pertneart September. If'n it snows early, it could come anytime, up there.'

'Wouldn't likely last, though, this early.'

'Might not. Might melt enough ya could git back out. Then agin, might close in an' stay bad all winter. Be tough to make it all winter if'n ya wasn't there all summer gittin' ready.'

Aware that it was, in fact, already the second week of September, Carver rode out before dawn. He packed more warm clothes and blankets than he thought necessary, as well as a lot more food than he should need. Just in case that early snow the mountain man had fretted about actually came, it might pay to be ready.

Riding past the fork in the trail that led into the Putnam ranch he pondered again the rancher's probing of his investigation. He seemed inordinately interested in what Carver knew. Might not hurt to check out that half-breed. Charley, that's what his name was. Charley White Man.

As he rode, he thought about Fast Dog as well. Every time he thought about him, the hair on the back of his neck rose. He could almost feel the Indian's eyes boring into his back. He resisted the urge to turn and look over his shoulder.

He spotted the deer trail leading up away from where two big cottonwoods stood. So far the mountain man's directions were perfectly accurate.

They continued to be. As if he had been there before, Carver followed the roundabout way into the hidden valley. As he topped out on the last ridge, he reined in his horse. He felt as if his breath had been taken away. Even Green's description hadn't prepared him for the majestic beauty of the scene that spread out before him. It was as if all the world were just practice for God's creation of this one perfect valley. Beaver dams had even created a small lake in the exact center of the valley. From where he sat his horse he could see the snow-capped mountains reflected in its still surface. It was the crowning touch of an absolutely perfect scene.

Carver knew he was silhouetted sharply against the sky. If Fast Dog were in the area, he was presenting him with a perfect target. If the Wild Thing were in the area, she would have certainly spotted him. Still, he couldn't move. He couldn't tear his eyes from the stunning beauty of the valley. He studied all of its length that he could see from his vantage point.

Along the creek he could see a black bear rubbing against a tree. On a green slope three quarters of a mile away half a dozen elk grazed.

Eventually, the alarms that his exposed position kept jangling in his mind overcame his appreciation of the scene. He lifted the reins and nudged the horse down the trail. Once he had descended far enough to limit the panorama of his vision, his caution returned. He quietly cursed himself for his lapse.

Almost a mile later he neared the bottom of the valley. He passed one of the trapper's cabins Green had mentioned. Still in purty good shape, he noted. Wouldn't take a whole lot ta make it liveable. Even got a big wood-pile yet. Thet'd sure be dry wood, though. At least it wouldn't smoke none.

When he'd gone 200 yards past the cabin, he turned to look at it again. Maybe the unexpected shift in his weight did it. Maybe it was just a loose rock. Maybe the steep side-slope in the trail just there was wet and slippery.

Without warning, Carver's horse went down. His feet slid out from under him, and he fell, hard, on his right side. Pain shot up Carver's leg. He yelled, and stuck his left foot against the saddle to try to pull his right leg from beneath the horse. Greater pain rocketed up his leg, and he stopped trying to pull it out.

The horse scrambled to his feet. He shook his head, making the bit-ring jingle. He snorted once, then stood still.

Carver lay still, waiting for the pain to subside. It came in waves, but the waves began to lower in intensity. He waited until they were at a manageable level, then he sat up. He moved the injured leg. Instantly the pain level shot up again, threatening to overwhelm him.

He swore softly. 'Busted it, sure's anythin',' he said.

He looked around. He was in a thick stand of timber. The old cabin stood 200 yards behind him. Aside from that, there was no shelter available.

'Now what'm I gonna do?' he muttered. 'They ain't no way I kin ride outa here with a busted leg. Even if I kin stay alive till it heals, by then it'll sure be too late to git out. If'n I don't die o' fever from the busted leg, I'll either freeze ta death or starve ta death.'

What form of death awaited him seemed the only options open.

'Well, jist as well die tryin',' he mumbled.

CHAPTER 9

Carver clamped his teeth. He steeled himself against crying out. He gathered his strength. He positioned his hands on his lower leg. He could feel where the bone was out of line. He had to get it back in line, before it began to swell. His right foot was wedged between two rocks. His left foot was braced against one of the rocks, ready to push. Holding his hands where he could try to force the bones into alignment, he heaved his weight back. He pushed with all his might with his left foot. He felt the bones slip into place. The trees above him whirled. Blackness overwhelmed him.

Consciousness returned slowly. Pain racked his leg. He felt sick. Sweat stood out on his face. He sat up. Pain rolled over him in wave after wave. He sat still until the spinning in his head stopped. He felt the leg. It was still lined up.

He leaned forward. Using both hands, he carefully lifted his right foot from where it was wedged between the rocks. He looked back over his shoulder.

A dozen feet away, dead branches of a downed tree jutted starkly into the air.

Using his left foot and both hands to propel him, he scooted backward toward the tree. By the time he reached it, the trees were spinning around him again. He closed his eyes, willing the nausea and dizziness to pass. Slowly, they complied.

He took the knife from its sheath at his belt and began to cut at the dead branches. It took him the better part of an hour to remove and smooth four pieces of branch. Each piece was about eighteen inches long. They were about an inch in diameter.

He shucked out of the leather jacket he was wearing. Using the knife, he cut half a dozen strips of leather from along the bottom of it. With the strips of leather, he bound the four pieces of branch tightly to his lower leg.

He lay back against the dead tree. Sweat poured from his face. He closed his eyes. After several minutes, he forced himself to move.

Using the downed tree, he hauled himself to his good foot. He hopped to where another dead branch lay on the ground. It was almost six feet long. Using it to steady himself, he began to hop toward his horse.

The horse's ears lay back flat against his head. His eyes widened. The grunting, hopping, wobbling apparition approaching looked far different from the man who had ridden him here. He sidled away.

Carver spoke to the horse. His voice was low, soft, soothing. It wasn't enough. The horse tossed his head nervously. He backed away.

For two hours he hobbled after the nervous animal. Periodically he leaned against a tree, willing the pain and nausea away. Twice he fell. Once he passed out from the pain as the fall put pressure on the fracture. When he regained consciousness, the horse still stood, well out of reach, watching him uneasily.

With a start he realized it was getting dark. He had not, could not, catch his horse. Without the provisions on the horse he would die. With the dark came increasing cold. In the last of the light he made out a low bank. Against it, wind and weather had piled two to three feet of pine needles, small branches and pieces of bark from dead trees. He hopped his way to it, laid down on the ground, and squirmed his way under the protective cover of the rotting vegetation. He scooped with his arms, piling as much of it on top of himself as he could. The exertion's warmth countered the chill of the ground. He stopped shivering. The pain in his leg subsided to a deep throb. He surrendered to the blackness.

Something moved against his leg. His eyes popped open. He reached down a hand. Something soft and warm jerked away from his probing hand. A mouse scurried from beneath the cover of piled debris.

Carver looked around. The sun was up. His horse was tied to a tree about fifty feet to one side. He started to move. Pain shot up through his leg. Memory flooded back.

He twisted his head to look at his horse again. Tied

to the tree, the animal pawed the ground with one foot, impatiently waiting. Carver sat bolt upright. He looked all around. Nothing moved within his field of vision. Somebody had tied up his horse while he slept. Who? Why? Where were they?

He swiftly assessed his situation. He could not ride. Even if he could somehow get into the saddle, he would be unable to ride far enough to find help. He would simply pass out from the pain and fall off. Then he would be back in the situation of being unable to catch his horse. The cabin! If he could get back to the cabin, maybe he could make it liveable enough to survive in it, while his leg healed.

But that would take at least a month. Maybe more. He didn't have that much food. Who had caught his horse for him? Was it the Wild Thing? Kylee, that's what her name was. If it was her. Who else could it have been? Would she stick around to help him? Would she bring him food? Would she kill him instead?

He shook his head. Too many questions. Not far away he could hear the creek, tumbling merrily over its rocky bed. Intolerable thirst prodded at him.

Using the same stick he had been leaning on the day before, he hobbled to the creek. He fell, more than lay down, just beside the stream. He dipped a hand in its icy water and washed his face. He rolled forward so he could use both hands. Scooping up handfuls of water with both hands, he drank thirstily.

He hauled himself back to his feet. The pain in his leg was echoed from every part of his body. He knew that by night the fever would begin. The more he hobbled around, tearing up flesh inside the leg with the jagged pieces of bone, the worse it would be. May not survive it now, he thought.

Making his way back to his horse, he untied the reins from the tree. The animal seemed less afraid of him today. Leading him, he made his way back to the abandoned trapper's cabin. The door still hung on heavy leather straps. It could still be closed. 'Cain't believe mice an' such ain't et up the leather,' he mumbled.

He tied the reins to a sapling close to the door. He stripped the pack and saddle off the horse, dragging them inside the cabin. He tied one end of his lariat in a bowline to his horse's leg, between hoof and hock. Then he led him toward a trickle of water he had seen seeping out of the side of the hill. Where that trickle spread along the ground, working its way toward the creek, the grass was lush and tall. The spring would provide the animal with plenty water. The lariat would allow a circle of movement with enough grass for a day or two. He tied the rope to a small tree, removed the bridle, and crippled his way back to the cabin.

Fighting the fever rising within him, he straightened things around in the cabin. He cleaned out the fireplace and set a fire, but did not light it. He arranged his bedroll on the single bunk built against one wall. He hung his foodstuffs from the ceiling, where rodents could not get at them. He ate the food he had kept out for his supper. It was within an hour of dark. Moving to the door, he laid a small wooden box he had found in the cabin on the ground, just outside. In the box he put some hardtack, jerky, and several pieces of dried fruit.

He moved back to the bunk and worked his way into his blankets. Exhausted by the fever that his body was trying hard to fight, he fell asleep almost instantly.

When he awoke, daylight was already flooding the cabin through the open door. He got up with great difficulty. His mouth was dry. He drank from the canteen he had left beside the bunk. He tried to drink sparingly, because he didn't think he could get to the creek again to refill it. His fever was too demanding. He drank long and deep. Shivering, he worked his way to the door. The food he had placed in the box the night before was gone. In its place was a freshly killed rabbit.

Relief washed through him. 'Well, at least I ain't alone,' he said aloud. He hobbled outside and skinned and gutted the rabbit. He hung it with his other food.

He lay back down on the bunk to rest for a few minutes. When he opened his eyes the sun was settling into the mountains to the west.

I slept the whole blessed day! he scolded himself.

He lit the fire that he had laid out the night before in the fireplace. From his food he got out three potatoes, some flour and some lard. He cut up the rabbit, floured and fried it. He used water from his canteen to boil the potatoes. Using the fryings from the rabbit, he made gravy with the remainder of his water.

It tasted like a feast. He quickly ate half of all he had cooked, placed the rest in the frying-pan and made his way to the door. He put it in the box. Beside the box he leaned his empty water canteen. 'Sure hope she sees fit to fill it,' he muttered.

He called into the woods: 'You oughter get this here food whilst it's still hot.'

He shut the door most of the way and hobbled back to his bed. He was asleep again within minutes.

In the morning the empty frying-pan remained in the box. The canteen that leaned against it was filled with fresh, cold water.

CHAPTER 10

The third day the fever peaked. His body was racked with pain. He shivered uncontrollably. 'Horse's gotta be outa grass,' he mumbled.

He fought his way out the door, staggering wildly on one foot and the long stick he clung to with both hands. Half-way to where his horse was picketed, he stopped. He had already been moved. Two circles of shorter grass betrayed where the horse had already grazed. He was picketed on a new patch of grass, still within reach of the trickle of water. Tears spilled unbidden down Carver's cheeks.

'Bless thet Wild Thing,' he blubbered, hating himself for his uncontrollable emotions even as he did.

He hobbled back into the cabin. Strange shapes passed across his field of vision and disappeared. Little flakes of black floated in front of him, then vanished. Shadows of strange birds passed in front of him. His shivering increased. 'I either got one awful fever, or it's turnin' plumb cold,' he muttered.

He hobbled back to the door. He looked up at the sky, surprised he hadn't already done so. A heavy bank of clouds was moving in from the north. The wind blowing out of it was dropping the temperature like a rock.

He hopped around to the wood-pile and began bringing in wood for the fire. He couldn't carry it, because it required both hands on the long stick to be able to hobble along. Leaning against the wood pile, he threw two dozen pieces of wood as far toward the cabin door as he could. Then he hobbled over to them, picked each one up again, and threw it further. It took him the better part of three hours to get the wood tossed inside the cabin.

He laid out a fire in the fireplace. He dug out his matches and laid them on the floor. He willed himself to start the fire. Outside, he could see snow already swirling in the air. He could not muster the energy to start the fire. He was shaking too hard to hold a match. He couldn't keep his thoughts together for more than a few seconds. He crawled to the bunk. He forced himself into his bed-roll. He lay there shivering so hard it rattled the bed. He couldn't stop. He couldn't think.

The temperature in the cabin continued to drop. The thought floated by that his canteen would be frozen solid by morning. It didn't matter. Someone would come to the office anyway. All that paper work would make a fine fire. It would be warm. Why was there a bed in his office? He couldn't make sense of that either.

His leg hurt so bad! His body ached with the fever. His head swam. He surrendered to the blackness again. He woke once. It was growing dark. Snow was already piled several inches deep on the cabin floor. He needed to shut the door. He couldn't remember where it was. He clutched the blankets closer around his neck. He drifted away.

He woke again. He was hot. Too hot. Eerie shadows danced across the walls. Smoke smelled faintly in the air. He frowned. Why would he smell smoke? Had he died and gone to hell? He lifted his head and looked around.

Strange animals danced around the room. Some had tails a hundred feet long. Some had four wings. Some had misshapen bodies he couldn't quite make out. The face of a gunfighter he had killed ten years before grinned from the head of one of the animals. The body of Will Tanning floated by, his head still dangling.

A woman laughed loudly. A man cursed. Sounds of a barroom brawl erupted, then faded. He looked up from the ground into the face of his horse, staring back down at him. Beyond the horse's head, strange clouds floated in the sky. A baby cried. An eagle screamed, but he couldn't see it. A squirrel sat on the foot of his bed, chattering busily. His head was too heavy to hold up. It fell back to the bed. He began to shiver again.

A hand slid under his head and raised it. Something pressed against his lips. Hot water. No, not water. Something bitter. The bitter liquid spilled into his mouth. He swallowed to keep from choking. More liquid. Swallow again. Again.

The hand lowered his head and went away.

Strange images continued to float about him for nearly half an hour. Then they began to fade away. The shivering subsided. He felt warm and safe. He ought to sleep. Yeah. Sleep. That was a good idea. He drifted into slumber, softly mumbling something, but he didn't know what.

He woke a few hours later. The strange shapes had returned. He was shivering again. The bed shook and rattled with it. Pain surged over him like waves of hot water, but it didn't warm him. He was so cold!

There was that hand again. And that bitter taste. Not hot now. Tepid. Still bitter. Swallow. Choke. Swallow again. Again. His head was lowered again. After a while the shivering subsided and the disconnected images ceased their parade along the walls. He slept again.

Daylight filtered through cracks in the cabin wall when he awoke. He was cold again. The crazy shapes and forms were gone, though. Nothing moved. He turned his head. A dark shape lay on the floor, near the door, wrapped in one of his blankets. He tried to speak. His throat was dry. Only a small croak emerged.

The instant he made the sound, the form by the door erupted. From the blanket sprang the wildest-looking human being Carver had ever seen. Her skin was too light for an Indian, too dark for a white person. Her hair was long and tangled. Bits and pieces of twigs, pine needles, and leaves clung in its snarls. Odd pieces of cloth and hide were loosely fastened to her body. They did little to conceal a strikingly shapely form.

Her eyes were wide, blazing with menace. Before her she held Carver's knife, pointed directly at him. She backed against the cabin wall, watching him intently.

Carver lifted both his hands, palms toward her. She relaxed only slightly. He pointed to the fireplace.

'Cold in here,' he said. 'I'll build a fire.'

Her eyes widened again. She shook her head frantically, but made no sound. With one hand she motioned him to stay in bed. Frowning, he complied.

Moving furtively, staying as far from him as she could, she circled to his canteen. She pushed it close enough for him to reach it, then backed away.

When she was back against the far wall again, he reached out slowly and picked up the canteen. He removed the lid and drank. He lay back down, holding the canteen beside the bunk. When he had rested for a few minutes, he raised himself up again and took another long drink. Then he replaced the lid and let it slide down on to the floor.

'Thank you,' he said.

He couldn't figure out why he was so tired. He'd said half a dozen words and taken two drinks. Now he needed a nap. He slept.

When he woke again, the girl was again asleep, beside the fireplace. Wind shook the eaves of the old cabin. It was cold. Bitterly cold. He wanted desperately to get up and light the fire. He knew that if he stirred the girl would waken instantly. He willed himself to stay put and go back to sleep.

Eerie half-light made forms in the cabin seem less than solid. A hand was on his shoulder, shaking him. He willed it to go away. It shook him again. He opened his eyes. The wild girl was standing beside his bed. His rifle was in her hand.

His eyes opened wider instantly. Alarms in his mind scattered the remnants of sleep. He started to say: 'Wha . . .'

She put a finger on his mouth. She moved the finger to her own mouth, in an unmistakable command to be quiet. She motioned him to follow her.

He struggled out of the blankets. It was cold! It must have been nearly zero in the cabin. His leg shot stabs of pain up his body as he moved it. He ignored the pain, forcing himself to stand. She handed him the stick he had used as a crutch. She pressed her finger to her lips again, and motioned him to follow.

As quietly as he could, Carver followed her. She moved silently to the door. She opened the door a crack, moving it very, very slowly. When it was open almost a foot, she pointed outside. She handed him his rifle.

He hobbled another couple feet forward and peered out the door. It was nearly dark. Snow lay three and four feet deep everywhere. Trees were bowed down under the weight of it. Bushes he knew had been there had disappeared.

Then he saw what she wanted him to do. Less than a hundred feet from the cabin, busily nibbling leaves from a bush sticking out of a snow drift, was a majestic buck mule deer. He lifted the rifle and thumbed the hammer back carefully, to keep it from clicking. He leaned against the wall, so he could stand without holding the stick. Some corner of his mind noticed the girl take the stick so it wouldn't fall and make a noise.

He sighted carefully at the deer's head. He couldn't hold the rifle steady enough. He was too weak. The front sight moved in a constant circle around and past the deer's head.

He moved the sight down, changing his aim to just behind the front leg. He had a lot more room for error there. He squeezed the trigger. The shot echoed from the mountains. A cascade of snow fell from above the cabin door. The deer jumped and fell sideways. It lay in the snow, kicking sporadically.

The girl took the rifle and handed him back his stick. She motioned him back to the bed. Carver started to protest, then thought better of it. The exertion of getting to the door and shooting the deer had expended his minuscule reserves. Fatigue washed over him. The room swam around him. He hobbled back to the bed and collapsed. The girl wrapped a blanket around her and went out into the brittle cold.

He didn't intend to sleep. He intended to lie down a few minutes, then get up and help the girl with the deer. They would need that meat. He just needed to rest, just for a minute.

The fire crackled merrily in the fireplace. Carver opened his eyes, aware he was uncomfortably warm. He raised his head. The hide of the deer was stretched on the floor of the cabin. On her knees, the girl was busily scraping the clinging tissue from the inside of it.

Carver noticed for the first time that the cabin's sole window was sealed up tightly with a folded blanket. He should tell her that was good thinking. She was busy right now, though. He'd rest another minute, then ask.

He didn't even realize he was asleep again.

CHAPTER 11

Slivers of bright sunlight filtered through those cracks in the wall of the cabin. It was warm. The smell of roast venison made his mouth water. He realized with a start that he was ravenous. He looked at the fireplace. There was no fire. He frowned. No charred wood remained. No ashes. Nothing.

The girl had a container of a white, milky substance. She was rubbing it into the well-scraped hide of the deer. Carver cleared his throat.

The girl sprang up from the deer hide and pressed against the wall of the cabin. Her eyes were wide open, but almost totally without expression.

'Sorry,' Carver said. 'I didn't mean to scare you.'

She did not answer. He wondered suddenly if the Indians had cut her tongue out. They did that sometimes, if a woman captive talked too much. Maybe that was why she never spoke.

She didn't drool, though. Somebody had told him women who'd had their tongues cut out drooled all the time. Something about the absence of a tongue made it impossible to swallow their saliva without tipping their head clear back.

'The venison smells good,' he said, taking care to speak very softly. 'I sure am hungry.'

Her eyes darted to the haunch of roasted meat lying on the floor. Wordlessly she picked up his knife, sliced off a chunk of the meat, and brought it to him. She laid it on the floor just out of his reach. Then she used the point of the knife to slide it closer so he could reach it, but not her. He picked it up.

'Thank you,' he said.

First time I remember eatin' off the floor, he thought.

Any hesitancy melted in the face of his demanding hunger. He bit off a chunk of the meat and began to chew. It was the most delicious thing he had ever tasted! He ate eagerly, avidly, pausing only to take swigs of water from the canteen that still leaned against the side of his bunk.

When he finished, he leaned back against the wall of the cabin.

'That was fine eatin',' he said.

The girl gave no indication she had heard him.

'What ya puttin' on the hide?' Then, after an instant's hesitation, he added: 'Kylee.'

Her head shot up. She dropped the pan of milky substance. Something flashed in her eyes. A sound, almost like a tiny sob, squeezed its way out from some spot deep within her. She stared at him for a long moment. After what seemed an interminable time, she responded.

'Kylee,' she said softly.

Carver grinned from ear to ear. He wanted to jump, to dance, to sing. Instead, he kept his voice soft and even.

'That's your name, ain't it, Kylee?'

'How . . .' her voice cracked, as if it hadn't been used for a very long time. She cleared her throat. 'How do you know my name?'

'Your Uncle Ralph and Aunt Dorothy come ta see me. They ain't never stopped lookin' fer ya.'

'For . . . for me?' her voice was tinged with an incredulous wonder.

'They been hopin' an' prayin' ya wasn't dead all this time,' he said. 'When they heard 'bout ya runnin' 'round the country, they come lookin' ta see if they could find ya.'

She whirled away and began furiously working the milky substance into the hide again. In the dim light of the cabin he couldn't be sure, but he thought he saw tears dripping into her work. He struggled to think of a way to continue the conversation.

'What ya puttin' on thet hide?' he asked at last.

Without stopping or looking up, she said: 'Brain. It tans the hide.'

'Thought that was prob'ly what ya was doin',' he observed. 'Brains work real good fer thet, long's ya don't heat 'em clear ta boilin'. Jist till they turn all milky thataway. Squaws teach ya thet?'

She stopped as if she had suddenly been turned to stone. Then she began rubbing the hide as though she were trying to rub a hole in it.

'Sorry,' he offered. 'Wrong thing ta say, huh?'

She did not answer. She continued to work in silence. Surprisingly tired again, he lay back down, but did not sleep. After while the chill began to penetrate.

'Guess I'd best build up a fire,' he said. 'Gettin' cold in here.'

She sprang up from the hide.

'No!' she said.

It was the loudest thing he had heard from her. He frowned.

'Why not? There's plenty o' wood out back, fer the time bein'. I kin hobble out there an' fetch some.'

'No!' she repeated. 'Not till dark.'

He frowned again. 'Why not?'

'He will see the smoke.'

'Who will?'

'Him.'

'Him, who?'

Her face contorted and twisted. She twisted her hands, wringing them together. Twice she opened her mouth to speak, then closed it again. At last she choked out the words: 'Fast Dog.'

Understanding flooded through Carver's still foggy mind.

'Ah! You don't think he'll be huntin' ya clear up here, do ya?'

She shrugged. All the hopeless despair of helpless victims stretching for endless ages echoed in the flatness of her voice.

'He will find me.'

'He's some sore 'bout ya gettin' away from 'im, all right.'

Her eyes jerked up to focus on his.

'You talked to him?'

He nodded. 'I wasn't sure who ya was. I'd heard a rumor 'bout him a-losin' a girl he'd captured in a raid somewheres. Took a Shoshoni named Lean Wolf an' Johnny Two Knives with me, an' traveled up an' talked to him.'

Her eyes flashed at the mention of Johnny Two Knives.

'He hates Two Knives,' she said. 'He is afraid of him.'

'Most o' the Crows is, I guess. That's how come I took 'im along.'

'You told him where I was?'

He shook his head. 'Naw. Didn't tell 'im nothin'. Just told 'im I'd heard 'e had a white wife, an' I wondered if it was a woman some folks was lookin' fer. Asked 'im if I could have a look at ya.'

Her voice was soft. 'What did he tell you?'

'He said he had one, but she'd been stole by someone. Said he knowed she hadn't jist run off, 'cuz she wouldn't never leave 'im by choice. Said he'd find ya, though. Said he'd carve up anyone what helped ya git away from 'im.'

'He will kill you when he finds me.'

'Naw, I 'spect not. Better men than him've tried it. I ain't gonna let 'im git ya, ya know.'

'Why?'

'Whatd'ya mean, "Why?" Why wouldn't I pertect ya?'

'You want to arrest me for killing Will Tanning?'

'Did you kill Will Tanning?'

Her eyes flashed again. He thought: She's gettin' right good at showin' emotion a'ready.

'No,' she said. 'He was a friend to me. He gave me food. He almost made me not afraid to talk for a little while. Then he killed him.'

'Who killed him?'

She shrugged. 'Fast Dog.'

'How do you know?'

'Because Will Tanning helped me. He found me. He came for me. But I wasn't there, so he killed Will. He had just gone when I came. I knew it had to be him, so I ran. I took a horse. Somebody followed me. It wasn't Fast Dog, though. He wasn't a very good hunter. I could always see him before he saw me.'

'Yeah, an' ya pertneart killed me twice!'

Her eyes opened wide. 'It was you?'

He nodded. 'It was me. It wasn't Fast Dog what killed Will Tanning, though.'

She scowled in confusion. 'Then who would kill him?'

'Now thet I don't know yet. But I'll find out. That's my job.'

'You are a . . . a sheriff?'

He shook his head. 'Deputy United States Marshal Carver Dilling, at your service, Miss Wadsworth.'

He thought she almost giggled, then the fear leaped back into her eyes.

'Why are you chasing me?'

'Well, there's a small matter o' someone wantin' 'is

98

horse back. Then there's a bigger matter o' findin' out who ya are an' what you're runnin' from. After your kin came, I knowed I had to find ya an' make sure thet danged Indian didn't never git 'is hands on ya agin.'

She pondered it for a long moment, then picked up a blanket.

'The horses need moving,' she said. 'I found a place where the snow blew off most of the grass.' She started for the door.

'Well, here! Wait a minute!' he demanded. 'Ya cain't go runnin' out there dressed like thet. Ya'll freeze ta death. Git some o' my clothes outa thet bundle over there. I brung extras, case it got cold. Why, ya ain't even got nothin' on your feet!'

After a long hesitation she opened his bundle of clothing. She put on one of his heavy wool shirts. It hung clear to her knees. She put on three pairs of his wool socks. She picked up the blanket again, wrapped it around her, and ducked out the door. In the brief moment the door was opened the cold swept through the cabin and set him shivering again.

CHAPTER 12

Carver didn't know he slept. One is never aware of being asleep, until waking. Then there is the knowledge of having been asleep, but sleep itself bears no awareness. Nobody really knows what being asleep feels like.

He woke with a start. Unaware of his actions, he swept the blanket off the arm holding his Colt .45. It pointed directly at the door, which had just opened.

Kylee stopped abruptly. Her eyes darted back and forth from the gun to Carver's eyes. He lowered the gun at once.

'Sorry,' he said. 'I musta dropped off to sleep.'

Wordlessly she moved inside and shut the door. Carver sat up on the edge of the bunk.

'The horses still OK?'

She nodded without answering.

He fought down a rising irritation. He wanted her to talk! He wanted her to tell him her story. He wanted to know what she was thinking. He wanted company and conversation.

'Still as cold out?' he tried again.

She shook her head. Then she turned to face him. She took a deep breath.

'It's turning warm, I think,' she said. 'The wind has changed.'

A dozen thoughts tumbled over each other in his mind. Warmer. Maybe the unseasonable storm was just an anomaly. Maybe winter wasn't setting in already. Maybe this early snow would melt into Indian summer. They might yet be able to get out of the high valley before winter.

'Think it'll melt the snow?' he asked.

She nodded.

He started to share the thoughts of escape from the valley, then changed his mind. Afraid as she was of Fast Dog, he wasn't sure she was ready to think about leaving even the uncertain haven of the valley she had found.

He probed his mind for ideas.

'How come ya decided ya could talk ta me?' he said eventually. 'Ya didn't never even talk ta Will Tanning.'

He thought a smile almost played around the corners of her mouth.

'Because your leg is broken. You cannot do anything to me yet.'

He considered the answer. It only brought another question.

'When did ya stop talkin'?'

She stopped what she was doing. She stood against the wall to one side of the fireplace, her back against the wall. Slowly she slid down the wall until she was sitting on the floor, her knees at her chin.

The blanket she had worn outside lay in a pile at her side. She still wore Carver's shirt that she had put on several days before. His three pairs of socks, still on her feet, were visibly wet. She seemed not to notice. She stared into his eyes in silence for so long he thought maybe she had forgotten the question. Then her eyes dropped. Her head moved forward until her chin rested on her knees. She wrapped her arms around her legs.

In a small voice he could scarcely hear, she said:

'The first time he . . . had me. I couldn't fight him. I tried. He just kept hitting me every time I tried to fight. He hit so hard! In the end I just gave up and let him. I knew he, or they, were going to do that to me anyway. The only way I could fight was not to let him know how much it hurt. So I didn't. I didn't cry. I didn't scream. I didn't say anything.'

'I'm sorry,' was all Carver could think of to say.

As if she had not heard him, she continued: 'It made him mad, that he could not make me cry. After a while he did it again, and he was rougher. He hurt me as much as he could. But I just lay there. I made up my mind that he couldn't touch me in my soul. He couldn't make me cry. He couldn't make me talk.'

'An' ya never did?'

'Never! Not one word. After a few days, he let some of the others have me too. I don't know why, but I belonged to him. I was his from . . . from . . . the beginning. They do that, you know. It is their right to let others have their women, if they want to. The woman belongs to them. Like a horse. It's all right to let someone ride your horse, if you say it is. So it's all right with their women, too.'

'Yeah, I know they're like thet,' Carver said.

'But they couldn't make me cry or talk either,' she continued.

Carver's voice quivered with intensity.

'You gotta be one tough little lady.'

She was silent for a long time. He did not interrupt her thoughts. He thought it must have been an hour later when she began to talk again. This time she started of her own volition, as if she had kept it all inside for far too long. She had spoken now. The dam was broken. All the backed-up, pent-up agony of four years of captivity had to be recognized. She told him of the attack, her terror, her grief at the deaths of her family, the brutal violation of her little sister. She told him of the endless weeks of captivity that turned into months, then into years.

'After a long time, I don't know how long,' she went on, 'I figured out I was . . . was . . . with child. I was sick a lot. But it didn't matter to him. He kept using me as much as he wanted. He kept making me work, and get whatever he wanted for him.'

'You could understand him?'

She nodded. 'I learned to understand them. I don't think I could speak it, because I didn't talk. I didn't practise saying anything, making the sounds. But I learned to understand.'

'An' he didn't even care if ya was sick?'

She shook her head. 'Even if I was, vomiting and things, he would just wait until I quit, and then he would, would use me again.'

She fell silent again, and he did not interrupt her thoughts.

'It was hard not to cry when he was born,' she said at last. 'It hurt so much! But I didn't. I didn't make a sound. Then I had somebody that cared about me. I had a son. He carried him around the village and showed him to everyone, because it was a boy. But I always got to keep him, because he wouldn't take care of him at all. None of their men ever do anything to take care of the children. They hunt. They fight. They use their women. That's all they do. They do not help with any of the work or with any of the children. Until a boy is old enough to learn to be a warrior. Then they teach him to fight and hunt and use women.'

His own heart echoed the bitterness in her voice, but he let her talk without saying anything.

After another long silence she continued.

'I made a very bad mistake, though. Even though I would not talk, I let him see how much I loved Caleb. I named him Caleb, after Caleb in the Bible. He was a strong, good man. He called him White Wolf, because he had the right to pick the name for a son. When he saw how much I loved him, he started using him to make me do whatever he wanted.'

'Usin' 'im, how?' Carver responded.

'He always wanted me to do many things that . . . that he could not make me do for him. I couldn't stop him from doing what he wanted to do to me, but he couldn't make me do things that their women do, that he liked. So he started threatening to hurt Caleb if I didn't. He would take him and hide him, so I couldn't find him. He wouldn't tell me where he was, unless I did what he wanted. Then he would go get him and bring him back to me.'

Again, Carver couldn't think of anything to say, so he said nothing.

She resumed her story. 'That's what finally happened to him. He was almost a year old. I knew when I had a chance to escape, I would have to take him with me, so it was going to be harder. But I still knew my chance would come. Then he wanted me to do one of those things again. Not for him, though. For another man. A really awful one. Even worse and dirtier than Fast Dog. Everybody in the village hated him. Were afraid of him. When I refused, he took Caleb again. But it was winter. It was cold. I knew he was really proud of Caleb, so I didn't think he would let anything really bad happen to him. Since he was almost a year old, he didn't need to nurse as often. So I still refused.'

A tear coursed down her cheek. When she spoke again, the feeling that was beginning to creep into her voice was gone. It was flat once more, without expression.

'I waited too long to give in,' she said. 'I finally realized he wasn't going to bring Caleb back until I did it. So I did it for him. Fast Dog watched. They both laughed a lot, and said all kinds of things about how he taught the white she-dog of a woman who was boss, and how to be a good squaw. When they were finished with me, Fast Dog brought Caleb back. But he had hidden him outside. He was frozen. My little boy was dead.'

Without even thinking, Carver slid on to the floor. Dragging his splinted leg, he scooted himself across the floor. He held out his arms to her.

She didn't see him for a long moment. She sat there, trying not to surrender to the flood of emotions that filled her. Her eyes were clamped tightly shut. She gripped her legs so tightly her arms quivered.

Then she opened her eyes and saw him in front of her, holding out his arms to her. She gasped once, and drew back against the wall. She seemed to melt. The stiffness drained from her. She flung out her arms and collapsed into his. She buried her face in his shirt.

He wrapped his arms around her and held her without saying anything. Great convulsive sobs began to rack her body, but no sound came out. Then, as if from someplace far away, a long wail began. It lifted out of the depths of a tortured soul, keened through a world of unspeakable pain, echoed back, surrounded them, wrapped them in its grief, then crumpled into heartbroken wails and heavy sobs.

She cried for her dead child.

She wailed for her lost innocence.

She screamed for the pain of a thousand violations.

She shuddered for countless humiliations.

She moaned for the family she would never see again.

She wept for her world that had been wrested from her.

She sobbed for the pain of wounds to body and soul that none could ever know.

She lamented all the lost dreams of her youth.

She subsided, at last, into mewls of woe for endless hours of unspeakable loneliness, isolated in the midst of a hostile and savage people, for a time that seemed without end.

Through it all, Carver held her. He murmured softly into the tangles of her unwashed hair. He ignored the small bugs that crawled across it, and sometimes on to his own face. He willed himself to bear the agony of his injured leg, stretched uncomfortably, racked by muscle spasms. He kept saying the only thing he could think of to say:

'It's OK now, Kylee. You're free now. It's all over. It's all OK now, Kylee. It's OK.' He said the words softly, over and over and over.

At last she lapsed into silence. Her breathing deepened. She began to snore softly. His back and arms ached intolerably. His injured leg went numb. Cold seeped through his back and arms and neck. He fought the need to shiver. He held her, let her sleep as the shadows outside lengthened. The tiny slivers of light that marked crevices in the cabin's wall dimmed and faded. Night settled.

Eventually he could stand it no more. He shifted his weight. She moaned softly, but did not move. He cleared his throat. She did not respond.

'Kylee,' he said softly. 'Wake up. We got ta build a fire. It's dark now.'

She stirred a little, as if to snuggle further into the warmth of his body. Then she stiffened. She jerked out of his arms and flung herself back against the wall of the cabin.

'It's all right,' Carver said, in the same soft, soothing voice he had spoken in for as long as he held her. 'It's jist me. It's got dark. We got ta build a fire.'

She blinked uncomprehendingly for the space of a dozen blinks. Awareness drove the sleep from her. She looked around, confirming it was night.

'I . . . I slept?' she asked.

'Ya slept purty good fer a while,' he agreed.

'You, you just held me?' she wondered.

'Ya sorta needed held some,' he offered.

He watched the wall of protection drop over her eyes, then lift again, then drop and lift again, as if she wanted to discard it but simply couldn't. At last she rose stiffly.

'I have cramps,' she said.

He rolled over and began to drag himself to the bunk. Agony shot through his injured leg. It was echoed by burning pain across his back and down his arms.

'Jist a mite cramped up myself,' he gritted.
'I will get wood and start the fire,' she said.
That sounded better than anything, just then.

CHAPTER 13

'You're plumb good at thet.'

Kylee looked up from her work. Sitting in the open door of the cabin, she was sewing a pair of moccasins cut from the hide of the deer he had shot.

'Where'd ya git the needle?' Carver asked.

'I made it from a bone of the deer,' she said.

'With my knife?'

She nodded, but did not speak.

'Well, what about the thread?'

'I pulled sinew from the deer when I dressed it,' she explained. 'It's what the women taught me to do. They use everything, when they kill something. They make tools and all kinds of things with the bones. They pull all the good sinew out, and tan it with the hide, so they can use it for thread. They even use the stomach, intestines, and bladder for water bottles.'

'I'd have ta be plumb thirsty,' Carver thought aloud.

She smiled faintly. It was the closest thing to a smile he had seen from her.

'When you get thirsty enough, it doesn't even matter whether they washed them first.'

'They let ya git plumb thirsty sometimes, huh?'

She nodded. 'And hungry.'

'But ya won,' he said. 'Ya never let 'em break ya. Ya never talked.'

Her needle stopped. She stared off across the valley. It was a long space of time before she spoke.

'But I can't go anywhere,' she said.

'Whatd'ya mean?'

'I can't go back there,' she said. 'I'd rather die anyway. But I can't go back home, either. My home is gone. My family is dead.'

'But they's all sorts o' folks that'd take ya in,' he said. 'An' your aunt an' uncle'd welcome ya.'

She shook her head. 'No. Not after I have been with the Indians. Especially when they learn I had an Indian child. They would hate me.'

'Naw, they wouldn't!'

'Yes. One girl did get away. She took her baby. She made it to where there was a wagon train. Mormons, I think. They didn't want her. In the end they said she could stay with them, but she would have to get rid of the baby.'

'They wouldn't let 'er keep 'er baby?'

Kylee shook her head. 'They wanted her to just lay it by the trail and leave it. She wouldn't do it. So they wouldn't let her stay there either. They gave her some food and water, and left her there.'

'What did she do?'

'She came back.'

'Ta the Crows?'

She nodded.

'Then what happened?'

'The one that owned her said he didn't want her any more. Then the rest of the men . . . took turns having her. Then the women beat her to death.'

For a long while he could think of nothing to say. Then he offered:

'Don't take kindly to captives gettin' away, huh?'

'It says the one that owned her wasn't man enough to make her happy, or to make her mind him. It is a really bad insult.'

'What happened ta the baby?'

She shrugged. 'They gave it to another woman to nurse. I suppose it just grew up with the others. It was a girl. When she is twelve or so, someone will take her for his woman.'

'Thet young?'

She nodded. She started to say something, then changed her mind. She went back to working on the moccasins.

'Snow's all gone,' he said, looking over the top of her. 'We'd best head out at first light.'

Her eyes darted to his. 'Leave here?'

He nodded. 'We got ta, ya know. There ain't no way we kin stay here all winter.'

'But you can't walk.'

'Naw, but I kin ride, by now. We each got a horse. We'll make it jist fine.'

'But, but what if . . . what if he . . .'

He cut her off. 'I hope 'e does. If'n Fast Dog shows

up, I'll give 'im a extra eye, right betwixt t'other two. Ya'll be safe with me.'

'But, but I have nowhere to go.'

'O' course ya do,' he argued. 'Now I kin see as how ya'd be uneasy jumpin' right inta town, amongst a whole bunch o' folks. But south o' Dubois, along the crick, they's a family I'm right good friends with. Merle an' Maude Garner's their name. Got a couple kids. Maudy's twelve er thirteen. Andy's 'bout ten. They'll give us a place to stay till ya feel comf'table.'

'Us? Will you stay there too?'

He pondered the question for a while.

'Well, yeah, I 'spect I will. I gotta hang my hat somewheres, till this leg gets healed up. Even then, it's gonna be stiff fer a spell, till I kin git it workin' good agin'. I 'spect they ain't no place I'd rather convalesce.'

'Con . . . valess?'

'Heal up.'

'Oh. I don't remember that word.'

'You remember a lot more'n I figgered ya would. Your ma musta taught ya good.'

Her eyes clouded. 'My parents both did,' she said. 'We read a lot. They were both educated people. They didn't want me to talk as if I weren't. I guess they never thought of me being a complete savage and living in a hide tepee.'

He thought she was going to collapse in tears again. He hadn't seen a tear since the day, several days previous, when she had finally broken. She had said nothing of that, and neither had he. She had begun to open up and talk regularly, but not about anything serious until now.

She shook her head. Her chin set. He offered what comfort he could think of.

'You stayed alive. More'n anything, I'm sure thet's what your folks woulda wanted ya ta do. I think ya did yerself plumb proud. Ya was a whole lot tougher'n I'da ever been, I know that.'

She shot him a grateful glance, then buried herself in her work again. After another long silence she said:

'Do you think they really would . . . accept me?'

'I know they would fer a fact,' he assured her.

'I'm afraid,' she admitted.

'Well, I 'spect thet's natural. It'll pass. You more scared o' them, or scared Fast Dog'll find ya, even there?'

'Both.'

'Well, put your mind at ease. Ain't neither one gonna happen.'

'I don't know how you can be so sure.'

'Well, I know the Garners, so I'm sure 'bout them acceptin' ya. An' I know me. There ain't no way in hell I'm ever gonna let thet danged Indian git his hands on ya agin.'

She stared at him for a long time. After what seemed like long enough to think up an answer to every question in the world, she said:

'Do you . . . do you have an extra gun?'

'An extra gun? What kind? You mean a sidearm like this?'

114

She nodded.

'Well, yeah. I got another pistol in a saddle-bag, over there in the corner. Forty-one caliber. Why? You wantin' ta have a gun?'

She nodded vigorously.

'What fer? Ta kill him, if he comes fer ya?'

She looked deeply into his eyes. 'Or for me, if he finds me.'

The thought shook him to the core. He tried to speak, but couldn't. He swallowed, but with difficulty. He lifted a hand and opened his mouth, then let it drop again. Then he hobbled over to the corner, opened a saddle-bag, and brought out a Colt .41. He checked the loads.

'You know how ta use it?' he asked.

She shook her head.

'Papa taught me to shoot a rifle. He never let me shoot his pistol.'

'Well then, we'd best teach ya. What'll we shoot at?'

'No!'

'Whatd'ya mean, "No"?'

'Don't shoot. If he's anywhere close, he will hear it. Sound carries too far.'

'Well, now, how ya gonna learn ta shoot it without shootin' it?'

'Take the bullets out.'

He thought it over. 'Well, all right.'

He emptied the gun, then showed her how it worked. He had her pull the hammer back to full cock, point it, and squeeze the trigger, then cock it

115

and squeeze again. He had her put it out of sight in her clothes, then pull it out and shoot. She practised until she felt she could handle it. Then he reloaded it.

'You be careful now,' he admonished. 'It'll jump in your hand somethin' fierce when ya shoot it fer real, so hold on tight. After we git outa here, down ta Garners, I'll teach ya ta shoot it fer real. But mind ya, I ain't givin' it to ya fer ya ta use on yerself. Jist him, if'n he ever finds ya. Which he won't.'

Before dawn the next morning, Kylee extinguished their fire. She brought the horses to the cabin. Carver's saddle she carried out and laid beside his horse. She did not know how to put it on. Her own horse, or rather, Grant Tucker's horse, had only a bridle. She folded her blanket and threw it on the horse's back.

Carver hobbled around the cabin, packing all of his things. When they were ready, Kylee carried them out. Using one hand and steadying himself with the other hand wrapped in his horse's mane, Carver heaved his saddle on to the horse's back. He instructed Kylee to go to the other side of the horse, be sure the saddle skirt wasn't turned under, and pass the cinch to him under the horse's belly. He cinched up the saddle, put his saddlebags in place, then secured his bedroll and pack behind the saddle.

'Gettin' on's gonna be the trick,' he muttered.

Looking around, he spotted a large rock. The top of the rock passed out of sight into the side of the gentle hill. The other side dropped straight for about two and a half feet.

'Kylee, see if'n ya kin lead my horse right up there alongside thet boulder. I'll hobble up on top of it, an' see if'n I kin git on from there.'

Using the same stick for a crutch he had been using since he broke his leg, he hobbled to the boulder. He sat down on it, then spun around and hoisted himself to his good knee, then used the stick to stand.

Kylee waited until his scrambling was finished and he stood on the flat top of the great rock. Then she led his horse over, positioning it right against the boulder. Carver took the reins. He gripped the saddle horn and swung his splinted leg over the saddle. He settled down into the seat, his right leg jutting out to the side.

'Kylee, see if'n ya kin pull this stirrup out there an' hook it over thet foot.'

Obediently she tried, but the stirrup wouldn't reach.

'Aw, jist as well, I 'spect,' he groused. 'I'd likely put weight on it an' mess the leg up. Well, I'll jist hafta sit flat in the saddle the whole way, I guess. Let's get movin'.'

Kylee went to her own horse. She leaped on to the horse's back as easily as hopping over a small stream. Carver led out and she followed close behind.

As they scrambled to the top of the first big hill, Carver pulled his horse to a stop. He removed his hat. While nothing showed over the top except his head, he carefully looked over the whole valley between them and the next ridge. Several elk grazed along a side hill. Nothing else moved.

Nodding, he nudged his horse on over the top and down the other side.

Topping the next ridge, he did the same, but nothing appeared out of the way. 'Six er eight more miles an' we'll be down along a road,' he called back to Kylee. 'Ain't likely to have no trouble then.'

She didn't answer. She was too busy watching every ridge-line, every tree, every bush. Because she was behind him, Carver was unaware that she rode with the Colt .41 in her hand, resting on the horse's back, just in front of her.

CHAPTER 14

Carver rode with his rifle across the saddle in front of him. His right hand held it, his finger on the trigger. His eyes darted everywhere.

His leg throbbed. He shifted in the saddle to try to ease the pressure on it. Pain stabbed along its length and up his back. As he shifted in the saddle, Kylee jerked the gun in her hand up, looking to see where he was looking. She lowered it again, and resumed her surveillance of the hills, the trees, the brush.

They followed the narrow deer trail that meandered down the last long hill before they came to the trickle of a creek that would eventually empty into North Fork. He rode directly between the two big cottonwoods that had been his landmark, and rode to the creek. He let his horse drink. Kylee hopped off her horse and let it do the same.

'Whole lot warmer here,' Carver said.

'Do you need to rest your leg?' she asked.

He shook his head. 'Don't wanta get off. Too hard gettin' back on. I'll likely stay in the saddle till we git there, if I kin.'

He wasn't sure he could. He noticed Kylee looking about nervously.

'We'll ride mostly in the trees an' such,' he said.

She did not answer. She simply stood silently beside her horse, waiting for him to resume the journey. Sighing in frustration, Carver reined his horse around. They picked their way along, staying where the trees would shield them from anyone watching from a distance. When there was a large open space, he tried to find a way around it that would keep them in the trees.

Three hours later the tiny creek emptied into North Fork. A road of sorts followed North Fork Creek.

'We'd jist as well stick to the road now,' he said, without turning around. 'Anyone lookin' fer ya ain't likely to be watchin' no roads.'

She did not answer, but he could almost feel her fear. She brought her horse up closer behind him. A tiny sound reached their ears. She wheeled her horse and plunged into the brush, just as Carver's head shot up. Following her lead, he reined his horse and jabbed the only spur he could use into his side. The horse followed Kylee's into the brush.

Twenty feet into the brush, both of them wheeled their horses and held them steady. They were well screened from the road, but with a fairly clear view through the intervening branches. Carver turned his horse sideways, so he could use the rifle without shooting over his horse's head.

Glancing over at Kylee, he was startled. She had returned to the same wild look of a hunted animal she wore when he first saw her.

'Easy, Kylee,' he whispered. 'Likely ain't nothin'.'

They waited almost five minutes before they heard it again. A horse's hoof clicked against a rock. A few seconds later they heard hoofbeats of a trotting horse. Half a minute after that, a cowboy came into view, his horse in a ground-eating trot, oblivious of two pairs of eyes that watched him ride past.

When he was gone Carver let out a long breath.

'I guess we're plumb spooky,' he said. 'If'n that'd been Fast Dog, he wouldn'ta been ridin' along a road thataway. We'd jist as well head down the road. We ain't likely ta see 'im now.'

Kylee's expression gave ample evidence of her disagreement, but she followed him back to the road. They resumed their trip.

Several miles later North Fork spilled into East Fork. There the road became wider and more used. Carver rode with greater and greater confidence. Then a new worry began to niggle at the corners of his mind. Most people in the area doubtless still believed Kylee to be the murderer of both homesteaders. If he was found with her, they would assume he was bringing her in, under arrest.

What mob action would follow the news of her capture he could not imagine. Certainly there would be crowds of the curious. Some would be afraid. Others would want instant justice. It was more than conceivable that he would have to face down a lynch mob.

As they neared the V–Bar–T ranch of Vince Putnam, he again led the way off the road, into the trees and brush. It was harder riding, but they needed to stay out of sight. He was in no shape to try to defend a prisoner, or to explain anything.

They rode carefully and furtively past the entrance to the ranch. They were three miles beyond it when he reined in sharply. Off her horse, as silent as a shadow, Kylee moved up beside him. In a large clearing, three cowboys riding V–Bar–T horses were ranged against a young man on foot.

The young man wore no gun. He held a rifle loosely in his right hand.

'What ya doin' on our range, homesteader?' one of the cowboys demanded.

'I ain't on your range,' the young man replied. His voice was casual, but strained. 'This here's gov'ment range. My homestead's jist down the crick.'

'This here's Vince's land,' the cowboy insisted. 'We been grazin' it since I been here.'

'Yeah, I know,' the young man agreed, 'but it's still gov'ment range.'

'You tryin' to pick a fight with me?' the cowboy demanded.

'I got no quarrel with you. But the facts are the facts.'

'Maybe you ain't heard 'bout homesteaders gettin'

killed hereabouts,' the cowboy suggested.

'If you mean Tanning an' Blount, I know about
'em. I heard it was likely it was thet Wild Thing what
killed 'em.'

'Maybe,' the cowboy said. 'Maybe not. Maybe they
jist thought they could crowd on to too much o'
Vince's range.'

'You ain't sayin' Vince done that, are ya?'

The cowboy laughed. 'I didn't say nothin' o' the
sort. O' course, now, if you was ta be found layin'
here with your throat cut, everybody'd figger it was
thet Wild Thing too, don't ya think? Then Frank,
here, he could jist naturally go an' file a quitclaim on
your homestead, finish provin' up on it, then sell it ta
Vince. I 'spect Vince'd pay 'im a tidy little profit fer
'is efforts.'

Carver lifted his rifle. He glanced around for
Kylee. She was nowhere to be seen. Frowning, he
turned his attention back to the four men.

'You mean you're fixin' ta kill me?' the young man
was incredulous. 'For my homestead?'

The cowboy turned to his fellows.

'Hey, boys, I think he's startin' ta catch on. Which
one o' you boys wants ta cut 'is throat?'

The young man started to raise his rifle, but before
he could more than move, three pistols were staring
at him.

'Don't even think about it,' the speaker admonished. 'Jist drop it.'

The man looked them over carefully. He was
clearly eyeing his chances. He had to know he was a

dead man, no matter what he did. Would he be quick enough to get one of them, or would they gun him down before he could even raise his rifle? His own chances were zero either way.

Carver centered the sights on the speaker of the three, just below his shoulder. Then, out of the corner of his eye, he spotted Kylee. Somehow she had slipped clear around the clearing. She had a stick in her hand. Screened from all four by brush, she was within six feet of one of the cowboys' horses, directly behind him. As Carver watched, still holding the bead on the cowboy, Kylee stepped forward. She jammed the stick, hard, into the horse just under his tail.

The horse let out a terrified squeal and lunged forward, nearly unseating his rider. He crashed into the horse next to him, causing him to shy violently to the side. The sudden clamor unnerved the first cowboy's horse as well. He lunged forward, crow-hopped once, then pranced sideways.

By the time the three riders had brought their mounts under control, the young man had them covered with his rifle.

'You boys best be droppin' them guns,' he ordered. 'I kin sure drop two of ya outa them saddles at least, afore ya got a chance o' gettin' me. I jist might maybe git all three. Now drop 'em!'

Two of the cowboys looked at the third, waiting for instructions. Their horses were still nervous, prancing. As they debated their chances, one of them came within range of Kylee's hidden position again.

The same tactic brought the same results.

Fighting frightened horses, covered by the rifle, the V–Bar–T hands conceded the strong hand to the homesteader.

'Drop 'em boys,' the leader ordered.

The other two were only too happy to do so.

'Now ride outa here,' the homesteader commanded. 'An' tell thet arrogant jackass of a boss o' yours that it'll be a cold day in hell when he gits Cody Weston's homestead. An' if I see any o' you boys anywhere's near my place, I'll shoot ya on sight. Now git!'

'You ain't heard the last o' this,' the spokesman of the cowboys promised. 'C'mon boys.'

He wheeled his horse and galloped out of the clearing. The other two followed immediately.

Cody Weston walked over and picked up the discarded weapons.

'Well, at least I got myself three mighty fine pistols,' he mused aloud. 'Now I wonder what spooked them horses thataway? You send a angel, did ya, Lord?' he asked, as he glanced upward.

The homesteader disappeared into the trees. Minutes later Kylee appeared as if by magic beside Carver.

'Now thet was some piece o' work,' he exulted. 'I'da sure never thought o' doin' thet. I was jist fixin' to buy in with my rifle, when I spotted ya. I didn't want any of 'em ta know we was here, though, so I'm plumb glad ya did it thetaway. Thet was somethin' ta see, thet was.'

Kylee did not answer. She simply jumped on to her horse and waited his instructions.

CHAPTER 15

'I, I can't.'

Carver reined in his horse. He turned the animal so he could see Kylee without twisting in the saddle. It just hurt too much to twist around.

It had been an interminable ride. The sun was just flooding the high valley with light when it began. Its course across the sky complete, that sun had long since gone to bed. In its place it had been kind enough to send a lesser light, but the moon was only a couple hours from settling complete darkness on to the land.

Carver had been off his horse once. Picking a good strategic spot where he would be able to remount, he had surrendered to his bladder's insistence. He had swung his bad leg over his horse, swinging himself to lie on the saddle on his belly. Kicking free of the stirrup, he slid down the horse until his weight rested on his good leg.

Without the stick he had used for a crutch, he couldn't even hobble. He stood there, hanging on to the saddle horn, to relieve himself. Then he called Kylee to lead the horse to a rock outcropping that would allow him to remount as he had mounted that morning.

By the time he was back in the saddle he felt totally exhausted. That had been hours ago.

'Ya can't what?' he demanded.

'I can't go there with you.'

Carver fought the urge to yell at her. He bit his tongue to hold back the words he knew were more fatigue and frustration than anger. He took a deep breath.

'Kylee, we been through all thet. It'll be fine. Ya got ta trust me.'

She shook her head. In the soft moonlight he could see her trembling.

'I . . . they . . . I don't want them to see me like this.'

'Like what?'

She bit her lip. She swiped suspicious moisture from her nose with the back of her hand.

'I . . . it . . . I haven't had a real bath, with soap . . . it's been so long. I have to look terrible. I smell worse.'

'You're plumb beautiful,' Carver said softly. 'Your hair could stand some combin', I'll allow. Ya ain't dressed the best. You're still beautiful. They'll understand. Ya got ta trust me. I wouldn't take ya there if I wasn't plumb sure.'

She sniffed. Her huge brown eyes bored into his, seeking assurance, hope. Her gaze dropped.

'I'm afraid.'

He nudged his horse over close to her. He reached out a hand and touched her arm. She jerked violently at his touch, then looked down at his hand. Her arm trembled beneath his touch. She reached her other hand across. The tips of her fingers touched the back of his hand.

Her eyes lifted back to his, then dropped again.

'It . . . that feels kind of nice,' she said in a low voice. 'I like for you to touch me.'

'It'll be all right,' he repeated. 'But we really need ta ride. I ain't gonna be able to sit this saddle much longer. Kin we go on?'

Her eyes came back to his.

'You're asking me? You're asking me if we can go on?'

'Of course.'

Her eyes misted over again.

'I guess I forgot what that was like.' She pulled her arm away from his touch. 'Let's get it over with.'

It wasn't nearly as bad as she feared. The dogs began to bark when they were a hundred yards from the house. By the time they rode up to the front door, a man stepped from the shadows at the edge of the house.

'Carver!' he called. 'We wondered if you dropped off a cliff or somethin'. Who you got with you?'

'Howdy, Merle,' Carver replied. 'I sorta did. Busted my leg.'

'What? You got a busted leg? Maude! Get out here! Carver's hurt.'

'Naw, I'm all right,' Carver insisted. 'It's healin' some a'ready. Merle, this here's Kylee Wadsworth. She needs you folks.'

'What? Who? Why, bless my soul! It's the Wild Thing!'

'Her name's Kylee,' Carver corrected. Turning to the girl he said: 'Kylee, this here's Merle Garner. Thet's Maude, comin' out the door. Gal behind her's Maudy. Boy's Andy. They're good folks. Ya don't need ta fear any of 'em.'

Kylee had slid from her horse's back. She stood beside it, trembling visibly. Maude approached her.

'Kylee, I'm Maude. Oh, my. You must be hungry. Do come in. Both of you. Andy, take care of their horses. Oh! Carver! You're hurt!'

'Busted his leg,' Merle explained.

'Oh, dear! Can you get down?'

'I kin git down. Cain't walk after I git there, though.' An idea flashed in his mind. 'Kylee, kin ya come an' let me put a arm around ya, so's I kin git inta the house?'

'Here, I'll take your horse,' Andy said, taking the reins out of her hand.

Hesitantly she walked over beside Carver. He felt her skin twitch and tremble as he put his arm across her shoulders. The feelings that coursed through him were what surprised him.

'Here, let me get the other side,' Merle offered.

He stepped over beside Carver, opposite Kylee. With the support of both, Carver one-footed it up on to the porch and into the house.

'Here, get sat down in this chair. How long it been busted?'

Carver saw Kylee eyeing the door. 'How long's it been, Kylee?'

Her eyes darted back to him. She opened and closed her mouth.

'Uh, seventeen. Seventeen days.'

'She found me,' Carver explained. 'I'da died. She caught my horse. Got me ta an old trapper's cabin. Big storm up there. We was clear up at the head o' Wiggin's Fork. I'da froze or starved. She plumb took care o' me.'

'We'll get Doc out here in the mornin',' Merle promised.

'Right now you need a bite of supper,' Maude insisted. 'Both of you sit down at the table.'

Kylee's voice was almost too soft to hear. 'I have bugs in my hair.'

Maude and Merle turned to look to Carver. Their eyes pleaded for him to say something to fill the sudden hollow of silence that descended on the room. Carver cleared his throat.

'Uh, Kylee's had a tough time. She got away from the Crow. They kidnapped her. She's been hidin' out in the hills. She ain't had a chanct fer a honest bath or a decent change o' clothes fer quite a spell.'

Maude's eyes darted back and forth between Carver and Kylee. She took a deep breath. She seemed to grow slightly taller.

'Well, we'll take care of that right after supper. But first, you both need a good honest meal. Then

131

Maudy and I will both help you. We'll heat water for the best bath you've ever had. We've got soap that'll kill every bug in there, guaranteed. Then we'll see about combing those tangles out of your hair. You just sit down there at the table, sweetheart.'

The meal was every bit as good as promised. The copper wash-boiler was set on the stove and filled with water, which heated while they ate. Then the menfolk were ushered out of the house.

'When we're finished, the water will be hot for your bath, Carver,' Maude announced. 'To be honest, you smell a lot worse than Kylee.'

'Ain't figgered out how ta git my boot off,' Carver complained as Merle got him settled down on the front porch.

'You ain't had it off since you busted your leg?'

He shook his head. 'Ain't had nothin' off. No way to git it off. Ain't sure how, even now. Sure hate ta cut it off. They's still good boots. But if'n ya pull it off, it'll likely mess up what healin' the leg's done.'

'Well, let's start with that splint you have rigged up on it. Then we'll just have to cut the boot off. Where's it busted?'

'`Bout half-way 'twixt the knee an' ankle.'

'Both bones?'

'Nope. Don't think so, anyhow. Jist the front one.'

'Well, it'll hurt some, but we'll try not to mess it up.'

It did hurt. But the bath felt wonderful! So did the shave and the clean clothes. Andy fell asleep, sitting in the corner. Carver felt almost new again. It did nothing to prepare him for Kylee.

When her bath was finished, she was spirited away to Maudy's bedroom. Sometime after midnight Carver, clean and refreshed, had struggled into clean clothes.

'Are you boys decent out there?' Maude called.

'Got clothes on, anyway,' Merle responded.

'Close your eyes,' Maude commanded.

'What?'

'Close your eyes! No peeking. We'll tell you when to look.'

Forcing himself to accommodate the request, Carver strained to interpret the rustling and giggles. After much too long, Maude said:

'OK, you can look now.'

Both men opened their eyes. Carver's eyes kept on opening, wider and wider. He fought to recognize what stood before him. Clad in a long nightgown of Maudy's a honey-skinned goddess glanced shyly at him, then at the floor. Her glistening black hair fell gracefully across her shoulders. Maudy's gown did nothing to hide the perfection of the shape within it.

'Kylee?'

Maudy giggled. Maude beamed. Kylee blushed.

Kylee raised a hand and brushed it across the soft flannel of the gown. Her voice was soft, wistful.

'It feels good.'

'It looks more'n good!' Carver exclaimed. 'You got ta be the most beautiful gal I ever seed in my whole life. Inside an' outside, Kylee, you're the most beautiful woman in the whole wide world, bar none.'

Kylee's blush deepened. Maude stepped forward and put an arm around her shoulders.

'We all need to get to bed,' she fussed. 'My word, it's almost morning already. Kylee, you can share Maudy's bed. Carver, you can have Andy's. You don't want to share a bed with that boy, believe me. He'll kick that leg of yours into pieces before morning. Merle, fix Andy a bed on the floor here in the front room. Well, help Carver in to the bed first. Andy's already asleep anyway.'

Kylee's eyes darted up to Carver's. They glanced toward Maudy's bedroom, then back to Carver, then to the front door, then the window.

'It's all right, Kylee,' Carver said quickly. 'We're plumb safe here. Even if he was anywhere in the country, an' even if he was tryin' ta track us, he couldn't in the dark. We're safe here. Jist relax. I'll be right in the next room.'

Maude's eyes darted back and forth between the two. A dozen unasked questions swirled about her. Carver shook his head slightly. Maude's lips compressed, but she said nothing.

Reluctantly, Kylee allowed herself to be led away to Maudy's bedroom. When Carver awoke in the morning, she was curled up on the floor between the side of his bed and the wall.

CHAPTER 16

'So who's after her?'

'Fast Dog.'

'Never heard of him.'

'Crow. His people live 'bout three days north. He's a bad un.'

'He the one took her?'

Carver nodded.

'How long did he have her?'

'Better'n four years.'

'Four years! You know what they say, Carver.'

'Yeah, I know. If'n ya kin git 'em back inside o' three months, they got a chance. After that they're damaged so bad they won't be nothin' but Indians or crazy.'

'It's true, too.'

'Not always.'

'What makes you think so?'

'I know 'er.'

'Not that well, you don't. You've only known her less than three weeks.'

'But I know 'er.'

'What makes you think she's different?'

'She never give in.'

'What do you mean? You mean they never raped her?'

'No, not that. She couldn't stop that. But she never let 'em beat 'er. Made up 'er mind right off not ta talk. Fer more' n four years, she never said a word.'

'What?'

'Not a word. Never cried. Never screamed.'

'For four years?'

'Fer four years.'

'That's incredible!'

'So's she. She's the most incredible woman I ever knowed.'

'And she managed to escape.'

'She got away. Hid out. Lived wild in the hills.'

'She kill them fellas?'

'Nope.'

'You sure?'

'Plumb sure. When Blount got killed, I was up in the hills, hot on 'er trail. She pertneart killed me twice, stole all my food from right beside me whilst I slept, an' I never caught 'er. But she was miles from where he got killed.'

'Well then! OK. But that means there's a killer out there, too.'

'Yup.'

'And you're laid up.'

'Fer a while.'

'What about – what was his name? Fast Dog?'

'What about 'im?'

'Will he come looking for her?'

Carver looked off into the distance. He sighed heavily.

'I'd like ta tell ya he won't, but I don't know. Kylee's sure 'e will. Chances are, she's right. Sooner or later, he's likely ta show up.'

'Then my whole family could be in danger.'

'Yup. 'Fraid so. Unless ya want me ta take 'er ta town.'

'She's scared to death of just my family. She could-n't stand being in town.'

'That's what I figgered. Town couldn't likely stand her jist now, neither.'

'Yeah, that's probably right. How long?'

'How long what?'

'Before Fast Dog shows up?'

'Maybe spring. Maybe never. Not likely in the winter.'

'Maybe before winter, though. I know you already had some winter up in the high country, but winter won't hit down here for another month or two. That's time enough for rumors of her whereabouts to get clear to him, easy.'

'Well, ya kin tell us ta git, if'n ya want.'

The silence was long and eloquent.

Then: 'You know, I might, if there were a choice. But there's not. We'll take our chances. But we'll go back to livin' like we did a few years ago. Have at least a couple guns in reach all the time, an' all that sorta thing.'

'I give her one, too.'

'Yeah, I know. Maudy told me. Wouldn't turn loose of it for nothin'. Made 'em leave it right there on the floor where she could reach it, even when she was takin' her bath. Kept it in the pocket of her nightgown.'

'Plumb s'prised she took ta the women folk so quick.'

'Just them, though. She won't let Andy or me within reach.'

'Wouldn't me fer a long while.'

'Don't seem afraid of you now.'

'Gettin' better. I guess she trusts me some. Thet the doc comin'?'

'Looks like. Now we'll find out what kind of bonesetter you are. See if he has to break it again to set it straight.'

'He better have a whole batch o' help if'n 'e tries.'

He didn't. He did order Carver to stay completely off it for another three weeks, then to work slowly into walking. Take walks. Use a cane while he needed to.

That suited Carver to a T. He didn't wait the whole three weeks. A full week short of doctor's orders, he and Kylee began to take walks, further and further from the house.

They talked. Around the Garner family, she still spoke very little. When they were away, she opened up and talked. She chattered. She giggled at his silly jokes. She helped him over rough spots he could have navigated just fine by himself, then kept hanging on to him much longer than necessary. He never objected.

After a bit they fixed a pallet on the floor at the foot of Carver's bed. She simply could not stay out of reach of his protection and sleep. Sometimes, after the others were asleep, she would slip up on to his bed and lie beside him. They talked in whispers until he fell asleep.

Three weeks after their arrival, she whispered to him.

'Carver? You asleep?'

'Nope. Jist thinkin'.'

'Will people ever accept me, do you think? After . . . you know.'

'Why would they need ta know?'

'What do you mean?'

'Well, they know the Wild Thing was found, an' sent to 'er folks somewheres. Thet's all I tol' anyone, 'cept Garners. They ain't gonna tell no one. You, now, you're a different person, named Kylee Wadsworth. All they need ta know 'bout you is thet you're with me.'

A long silence followed. Then she said: 'Do you think you could ever forget?'

'Fergit what?'

'What . . . you know.'

' 'Bout the Indians an' all?'

'Yes.'

'I a'ready did.'

'Really?'

'Really.'

'It doesn't bother you?'

'Only thing bothers me is bein' this close to ya, an' being afraid ta touch ya.' Silence again. Then he heard the rustling of cloth. Then the covers lifted, and she slid into bed beside him. Her hand found his. She brought it over on to her body. He started wide awake with the realization that she lay naked beside him.

'I think it would be completely different for you to touch me,' she said softly. 'I . . . I want you to touch me. To love me. I need to know that I'm not loathsome to you.'

She was anything but that. He had been hopelessly in love with her for a month, and afraid to say so. He certainly let her know it now.

The passion with which she responded left him breathless.

The leg was completely healed and strong quite a while before he would admit it. He just didn't want the time to end. His duties as Deputy United States Marshal were on hold. The unsolved murders were far away. Winter settled in, but mildly, for that country. There was little snow. What fell soon thawed on the sunny slopes. People began to talk about Christmas.

Then the rider came.

Carver and Kylee were just leaving the yard. Both wore winter coats, but no gloves. The day was clear and bright.

With the first sound of the running hoofbeats, the old fear leaped instantly into Kylee's eyes. Carver laid a hand on her arm. He led her behind the corral fence, where they could see the approaching rider. He wasn't even aware his gun was in his hand. Kylee was very much aware that hers was.

CHAPTER 17

'Marshal! Marshal! Marshal Dilling! Where you at?'

The rider skidded his horse to a halt and leaped from the saddle. Merle stepped out of the house, gun in hand.

'What's the problem?'

'They's been a killin',' the rider proclaimed. 'I need to see the marshal.'

Carver stepped from behind the corral. Kylee stayed close behind him.

'I'm right here. Who're you?'

'Blake Dabney. Got a homestead up East Fork. My neighbor got killed.'

'Who's your neighbor?'

'Cody Weston.'

'Ah!'

'You know him?'

'Met 'im. How'd 'e get killed?'

'Somebody cut his throat. Ear to ear! It's awful, Marshal! He didn't even see who did it, I don't think. His gun's still in the holster. Right in front of his outhouse. Like he just came outa the outhouse, an'

someone come up behind him an' cut his throat.
Musta been that Wild Thing again.'

'No, it wasn't.'

'Huh?'

'I said it wasn't the Wild Thing.'

'How do you know that?'

'Because the Wild Thing was just a girl who
escaped from the Indians, and was scared to death,
hidin' out in the hills. She's been found an' brung
home. She ain't out there no more. She didn't kill
nobody.'

'What? Are you sure?'

'Dead flat plumb sure. An' ya kin pass thet word
around, too.'

'So where is she? The Wild Thing, I mean.'

'With folks what love 'er, an' thet's all ya need ta
know. Jist make sure folks know she ain't the one
done none o' the killin', an' she ain't out there no
more.'

'Well, all right. If you say so. But who's doin' it
then?'

'Now, thet there's my job to figger out, ain't it? An'
I 'spect I got it figgered. You'll know, soon 'nough.'

'Well, all right. If you say so. You want me to ride
back to Cody's with you?'

'I'd be obliged. You best git your horse rubbed
down some, though. Ya rode 'im kinda hard. I got
another horse out here I gotta take back to Grant
Tucker, too. Ya kin ride him, ta give your horse a
break. He's in the barn. Buckskin geldin'.'

Blake led his horse to the barn. Kylee searched

Carver's face, panic in her eyes.

'I have to go with you.'

He shook his head. 'No. Too dangerous.'

'It's him, isn't it?'

'Who?'

'Fast Dog.'

'No.'

'How do you know?'

' 'Member them fellas that was bracin' Cody in thet clearin'? When ya jabbed one o' their horses in the . . . uh, when ya jabbed thet horse?'

She nodded.

'They tol' 'im they'd kill 'im. I 'spect they did. Or had one o' Putnam's boys do it. I 'spect I know which one.'

'Putnam?'

'Vince Putnam. Owns the V–Bar–T. He's tryin' ta run out the homesteaders an' take over their claims, so's 'is ranch won't lose all 'is grazin'.'

'What will you do?'

'I got ta ride up there an' have a look. See what I kin find.'

'I want to go with you.'

'Not a good idee.'

'I don't want to stay here without you.'

'Yeah, I know. But it's safer thetaway. I'll be back today er tomorry.'

He had to keep from looking at her as they rode out of the yard. He knew he could not leave her there if he had to see the look in her eyes.

The scene at Cody's homestead was as grim as the

other two had been. The young homesteader lay on his back. His throat had been slit from ear to ear. Blood covered the whole area around him.

'Never even drew his gun,' Blake lamented.

'Somethin' in 'is hand,' Carver said.

'Huh?'

'His right fist is clenched up. Looks like somethin' in it.'

'Yeah! There is! But he's stiffer'n a board. How you gonna get his hand open?'

'Pry it open, I 'spect.'

Blake had to turn away as, one at a time, the lawman broke the homesteader's fingers to open the clenched fist. When he had the hand open enough, he extracted a narrow strip of buckskin with beadwork attached, tightly wadded.

'Gotcha!' he said.

'What is it?' Blake asked.

'The name o' the killer,' Carver replied.

'Huh? I don't see no name.'

'Jist as well be. I seen it afore. I know who wore it. Cody managed to grab the fella's wrist. He got aholt o' the end of 'is sleeve, an' didn't let go, even when 'e died.'

'You know whose that is?'

'Yup.'

'You gonna get up a posse?'

'Yup. You got a family?'

'Uh, yeah. I got a wife an' a little girl.'

'Good. Go home. I'll take care o' this.'

'You sure?'

'I'm sure. Now git.'

Carver mounted his horse and headed for Dubois. He made seven stops, delivering the same message and instructions at each stop. On the way past the post office, the postmaster called out to him.

'Hey, Marshal! Long time no see. You OK?'

'Yeah, I'm fine, Wally. Been laid up with a busted leg. Figgered ya'd heard.'

'Well, I had, really. Heard you were out at Garners, getting healed up. Heard you found yourself a right good-looking woman, too. She must be pretty hard up to take a shine to you. You look fine.'

Carver grinned. 'I'm fine. All healed up. An' you're right 'bout her bein' one fine-lookin' woman.'

'Well, you got a whole pile of mail in here. You want it yet?'

'Naw. Let it set a while longer. I got some business ta deal with.'

'That so?'

'I 'spect y'll hear 'bout it tomorry.'

'Not gonna tell me, huh?'

'Tomorry, Wally.'

Tomorrow. The knot in his stomach said there very well might not be tomorrow. He didn't understand that. His plan was sound. It should present no problem. Then why should he feel the cold fingers of death playing games with his spine?

CHAPTER 18

The good weather was over with, it seemed. The north wind sent shivers through his sheepskin-lined coat. Its tendrils reached inside his gloves, numbing his fingers. It seemed to freeze his hand to the grip of the double-barreled shotgun.

Dark clouds matched the menace he felt in his bones. The mountain peaks were hidden behind the gray curtain. 'Snowin' hard up high,' he muttered.

At the entrance to the V–Bar–T ranch yard he stopped his horse. Standing in the stirrups, he studied the layout of house and yard. Several times he studied a spot carefully for a long while, then nodded and moved on. Satisfied at last, he lifted the reins and rode into the yard.

Dogs came out of the warmth of the barn to herald his arrival. He smiled tightly.

'Cold came at the perfect time,' he muttered to his horse. 'Dogs was all hidin' out in the barn, lettin' the horses keep 'em warm.'

It was clear they weren't yet accustomed to the

weather. Warm days had held so long into the winter, they hadn't had the chance. This was the first real cold snap. After the obligatory heralding of his arrival they retreated, tails between their legs, to the relative warmth of the barn. 'Musta dropped fifty degrees since yesterday,' he said.

In front of the house, Carver turned his horse sideways to the front door and waited. He didn't wait long.

The door opened, and Vince Putnam stepped out. Right behind him, Charley White Man slid through the door and posted himself at the rancher's left.

'Mornin', Marshal,' Putnam greeted him. 'Get down an' come in?'

'Not today, Vince.'

'Here on business?'

'Yup. Charley, you're under arrest.'

'Me? What for?'

'Murder. I'll be askin' ya to put your hands up.'

'Now just a minute, Marshal! Are you saying my right-hand man murdered somebody? Who?'

'Cody Weston, last. An' afore that, Simon Blount. Afore that, Will Tanning.'

Charley eased half a step further from the rancher. His hand hovered above the butt of his gun. Putnam held up a hand.

'Easy, Charley. Now, Marshal, you gotta be mistaken. Charley, he ain't hardly been away from the ranch. He's sorta my personal bodyguard. He's with me, pertneart all the time. There ain't no way he could murder someone and me not know about it.'

'Yeah, that's what I figgered too,' Carver agreed.
' 'Specially after I listened ta three o' your boys fixin'
to kill Cody Weston. They would've too, if I hadn't
been there.'

Vince and Charley exchanged looks.

'Whatd'ya mean? You was there?'

'I was sittin' in the trees, fixin' ta even up the
score,' Carver amplified. 'Didn't need to, though.
Seems one o' your boys' horses got a stick rammed
under 'is tail all unexpected. Sure gave Cody a
chance to git the drop on your boys.'

Vince and Charley exchanged the look again. A
silent message visibly passed between them. Vince's
demeanor changed noticeably.

'So that's what happened. The boys told me one o'
the horses squealed and rammed into one o' the
others. Sorta kept 'em all three busy just handlin'
their horses for a minute or two.'

'Long enough,' Carver agreed.

'How'd you do that?'

'Don't matter none. What matters is thet your
racket's all done. It's out in the open. Thet's why
you're both under arrest.'

'Both of us? Now you do have a high estimation of
your ability, Marshal.'

'It'll stand. Now I'll be askin' ya both to lift your
hands.'

'Just one more thing, Marshal. You said something
about proof. If you have any proof that Charley or I,
either one, had anything to do with those murders,
I'd sure like to hear it.'

Carver held out his left hand. Dangling from his gloved fist was a narrow strip of buckskin, with tiny, bright-colored beadwork attached.

'I 'spect this is yours, Charley.'

'What? What's that?'

'Part o' your buckskin shirt. The beaded one. The one you pertneart always wear. Cody got ahold of it. Tore off a piece. I recognized it, 'cuz it's the one ya was wearin' last time I seen ya.'

Charley stared at the thin strip of condemnation. Then he began to swear furiously. Vince held up his hand again.

'Well, that's really too bad, Marshal. I guess you got us dead to rights. Too bad you'll never live to tell anyone, though.'

He lifted his voice. 'Boys, step out and show the marshal what he's up against.'

Immediately half a dozen hands stepped into view. Each held a rifle, pointed at the marshal.

Vince smiled. 'I'd've thought you'd had better sense than to ride in here like that, and think you could just arrest both of us, Marshal. I'm disappointed. I thought you were a smarter man than that.'

Carver shrugged. 'We all make mistakes. Ya really don't think ya kin git away with it, do ya, Vince? Folks around ain't thet dumb. When folks see ya snapped up all the homesteads right away, soon's the fellas what filed on 'em got killed, they'll put two an' two together.'

Vince chuckled again. 'Just coincidence, Marshal.

Besides, everyone in the country knows it's that Wild Thing runnin' around the hills that killed all three of them.'

Carver shook his head. 'No, they know better. The Wild Thing, as ya call 'er, has a name. I found 'er. She's back with folks what'll take care of 'er. She wasn't runnin' around no more a'ready when Charley killed the last two fellers.'

Vince and Charley exchanged another quick look. Then Vince shrugged.

'Well, it doesn't really matter. The only one that knows that is you. And it doesn't look like you're likely to live out the day, Marshal.'

'Are ya sayin' ya plan ta shoot me, Vince? In cold blood?'

Vince laughed softly. 'Why not? One more sure ain't gonna make no difference is it?'

'Yeah, I guess four ain't much different than three,' Carver agreed.

'There'll probably be a couple or three more,' Vince boasted. 'There's about that many more homesteads I really need, to have a lock on the water. After that, I'll pretty well control the valley. It's survival, Marshal.'

'Yeah, well, I sorta like ta survive too, Vince.'

Carver stood in his stirrups.

'You boys kin show yerselves now!' he called out.

Putnam's eyes widened. Charley's narrowed. Both shot quick glances around the yard. From behind the corners of every building in the yard, and from a couple trees close to the yard, men stepped into view. Each had a rifle trained on the men in the yard.

Putnam's gun hands sized up the situation instantly. Every one of them slowly lowered his rifle to the ground and stood, hands raised.

Charley cursed. His hand was only slightly faster than Vince's, as both of their guns streaked from their holsters.

The shotgun in Carver's hands bellowed. Charley doubled in the middle and was lifted two feet backward. Half a dozen rifles barked at the same instant. Putnam's bullet-riddled body flopped backward. His head landed just across the threshold of the open door.

Carver turned to survey the yard. Every man in the yard stood with his hands as high as he could reach.

'Gather 'em up, boys,' Carver called out. 'Herd 'em inta town. If any of 'em makes a break or tries anythin', drop 'im in 'is tracks.'

Following his instructions, the men Carver had recruited the night before in town began to herd the prisoners to the barn to saddle their horses. It would be a long, cold ride to town.

Even colder were those fingers of death playing with Carver's spine. He frowned his confusion. It was over. Putnam was dead. Charley White Man was dead. Any of Vince's men who escaped the round-up would hightail it out of the country in a hurry. Then why did he have the overwhelming sense of impending doom?

He carefully reloaded the shotgun. He shook his

head. The feeling would not leave. He had felt it too many times to argue. He lifted the reins and rode to meet whatever lay ahead.

CHAPTER 19

The collar of his coat was pulled as high as he could keep it. His hat was pulled down against it. Even that failed to make any pocket of warmth around his neck and ears. Any warmth that was there, the bitter wind snatched away, leaving only the cold that made his ears ache.

His fingers were numb again. It should have been warmer with the wind at his back. It didn't seem to help. His makeshift posse and their prisoners were on the way to town. He wanted only to get back to Kylee. Another hour and he'd be with her. It was only yesterday he had left her at the Garners. It seemed like for ever.

He wiggled his toes in his boots. They hurt with the cold. His leg, still freshly healed at best, throbbed with the cold. The wind's icy fingers reached up his nose, and their touch stung and smarted.

'Must be twenty below or better,' he muttered.

He would have seen him quicker if it hadn't been so cold. He had already been in the saddle since before sunrise. He wasn't conditioned to it yet. He had been loafing, healing, too long.

It was the cold that forced him to hunch down into his coat. The cold kept his head down, trying to hoard just a little of his body heat to keep his face from freezing.

He wouldn't have seen him then, if his horse hadn't reacted.

The horse's ears went forward. His head lifted slightly. He didn't really snort. It was more like he just blew his nose a little.

It was enough to alert the lawman. His head jerked upright. It was too late. Sitting in the road directly in front of him, mounted on a black-and-white speckled horse, sat Fast Dog. An old army blanket was wrapped around him. Peeking out of the blanket was the unmistakable blue of a gun muzzle.

As if he had seen him all along, Carver continued on his course. He continued until he was less than twenty feet from the Indian. Then he reined his horse so the animal's head was not between him and the warrior.

He nodded. 'Fast Dog.'

'Where my woman?'

'You got a woman? If she's your woman, I 'spect she's at your village. If she ain't there, then I 'spect she ain't your woman.'

'White woman my woman. I come for her.'

'Well, I 'spect you'll jist have to go back without 'er. She ain't your woman. Ya stole 'er. Ya abused 'er. Ya treated 'er like dirt. You're plumb lucky she ain't here, or she'd blast ya right offa thet horse.'

'I take woman back.'

'Only thing you're takin' back is your hide, if'n you're lucky,' Carver disagreed.

He knew that beneath the blanket the Indian had his finger on the trigger of his rifle. He also knew his own hand was so numb with cold he might not be able to squeeze the triggers of his shotgun. Well, at least now he understood what the premonition was.

'Then I kill you. Then I find,' Fast Dog said.

There was only the tiniest hint of movement beneath the blanket. It was all Carver needed. With every ounce of determination he could muster, he forced his numbed fingers to jerk against the triggers of the shotgun.

They responded. They were too numb to pull just one trigger. They pulled both.

The double load of buckshot barreled into the Indian, propelling him backward off his horse. His rifle discharged into the air as he was driven backward. He landed in the road, sprawled on his back. He did not move.

Carver edged his way to the Indian's nervous horse. After several attempts, he managed to catch the rope from the crude hackamore that passed for a bridle. He shoved his hands inside his coat, hugging his sides until they warmed enough to use them. He reloaded the shotgun. He lifted the reins and set out on a swift trot, leading the other horse.

It was less than an hour to the Garners. As he rode into the yard, Kylee came flying out to meet him.

Then she spotted Fast Dog's horse. She stopped so abruptly she almost fell on her face. Her fear-filled face turned up to him.

'He's dead,' Carver said softly. 'I killed 'im. He ain't gonna never hunt ya no more.'

She looked back and forth from the horse to Carver for a full minute.

'Where?'

' 'Bout five miles back.'

'Is he still there?'

He nodded. 'Didn't seem no hurry dealin' with the body. He'll be froze a'ready.'

She looked long into his face.

'I want to see him.'

'What? You sure?'

'I have to.'

'Well, you go git some warm clothes then. I don't want ya freezin' ta death on me.'

She whirled into the house and returned in less than a minute. She carried two blankets. She hopped on to Fast Dog's horse. She wrapped the blankets around her, then kicked the horse into action.

Shrugging, Carver followed.

She approached the body slowly. She rode a complete circle around it. She slid from the horse. She sidled up to the body. She kicked him. He was already frozen stiff. She kicked him again to be sure.

Dropping to her knees, she snatched a knife from the dead Indian's belt. With a squeal that sounded more animal than human, she plunged it into his chest. She withdrew it and plunged it back again and

157

again, making that strange noise between a scream and a groan.

Carver stood stupidly in the road, not knowing what, if anything, to do.

Then she moved slightly and began sawing at the dead man's throat. With surprising ease, she severed the head from his body. She dropped the knife in the road and leaped to her feet. Carrying the head by its hair, she lunged into the brush.

Hurrying behind her, Carver was just in time to see her take both hands and throw the head as far out into the river as she could heave it. Then she stood there, shaking.

He walked up behind her.

'Feel better?'

She whirled toward him. Her face contorted with fear, with rage, with loathing, with the toll of four years of torture and abuse. Then the tears came. He held out his arms. She came into his arms, burying her face against him, and sobbed. He couldn't understand anything she kept saying. He didn't need to. He just held her.

After a time the cold overcame the surging rush of her pent-up feelings. Her shaking changed from emotion to just plain shivering. He turned her toward the road.

'C'mon. We gotta git ya wrapped up in them blankets, afore ya ketch your death.'

She allowed him to lead her back past the headless body in the road. She leaped on to the horse. He handed her the blankets. She wrapped them around herself, borrowing the horse's heat as well as the blankets' protection. After a few minutes her shivering slowed.

'Why'd ya do thet fer?' he asked finally.

A shudder passed through her.

'It is what I dreamed of being able to do one day,' she said, in a small voice. 'To stop being afraid of him. To know he can't even look for me from beyond his grave.'

'An' thet'll keep 'im from it?'

'I don't think it matters. I think he was in hell the minute you shot him. But he would believe that. The Crow fear Johnny Two Knives because he does that. He cuts off their heads, and hides them somewhere they can't be found. They believe that unless his people, especially his wives, can find his head and bury it with him, he will spend eternity wandering, without being able to see or hear or eat or anything. It's their version of hell, I guess. I made up my mind a long time ago that if I ever got the chance I would see that he got to live as much hell as he made me live.'

Silence hung in the frost-laden air for several minutes. She looked at him for a long moment, then dived off the horse into his arms. He held her there, in the middle of the road, beside the dead and headless body of her tormentor. Then she pushed away from him.

'There's one more thing I want to do.'

'What's thet?'

'I want to send him home with a message to his

people. I want them to know it isn't all right to kidnap and rape people.'

'What'cha got in mind?'

She showed him, instead of told him. She picked up the knife again and sliced off the clothing from the Indian's groin. Then she deftly sliced his manhood away. That with which he had tortured her so relentlessly now lay in the frozen road.

'Now, let's tie him on his horse, on his back, so everyone can see what was done to him, and let his horse take him home.'

A shudder passed unbidden down the length of Carver's body. He shrugged. He muscled the Indian's mutilated body on to his horse, face up. Then he used ropes to pry the reluctant corpse downward at hands and feet, until he could tie him securely. The effect was profoundly gruesome.

Removing the horse's crude hackamore, he turned it in the direction of home and slapped it on the rump. The horse galloped off for about fifty yards, then slowed to a trot. He knew it would go unerringly home.

'Ya all right now?' Carver asked.

She sighed heavily. Then she nodded.

'Yes. I think I will be all right now. If you don't ever leave me again.'

He smiled suddenly. 'Now thet's somethin' I sure don't intend ta do any more'n I gotta.'

Somehow, he didn't think he'd need to be gone from home very much at all.